BAA-BAA BAD MEDICINE

FARM FRESH COZY MYSTERIES, BOOK 6

SUMMER PRESCOTT

SUMMER PRESCOTT BOOKS PUBLISHING

CHAPTER ONE

"I'm not sure I understand how you make a living, Mom."

Christopher Beaumont stood on the porch of his mother's two-story farmhouse and surveyed the acreage in front of him. His mother, Shea, stood next to him and gazed out at the land. To her left was the new metal barn that had been erected after her old barn had burned to the ground.

In the field surrounding the barn was another small outbuilding that had been added since her purchase of the farm two years before. A herd of goats occupied the two-acre field which ringed that building. Beyond that, were rows after rows of maturing corn, planted by Barry Demarcus, her best friend's husband.

A gravel driveway divided the farm in half, with a smaller barn, her vegetable garden, a chicken coop, two greenhouses, and her house on the opposite side. To Shea, it had become her own little slice of heaven, despite the hard work she had to put into it year-round. But she could imagine how it might look to her children, who had grown up in suburbia. Christopher seemed interested in her financial security while Carrie, his twin, had fairly quickly sequestered herself inside the farmhouse to use the internet and her phone. Unfortunately, she'd made it terribly evident that she hadn't exactly been excited when she first saw the charming little farm.

Shea could read the fields like a book and had learned more about farm life since she'd arrived than she'd ever dreamed possible. She preferred the Blue Lake variety of green beans over the pole beans and could taste the difference. She also knew which kinds of tomatoes were best for making sauce, and which ones – when you sliced them up and ate them fresh – would make your eyes roll back in your head with their sweetness.

She'd not only learned how to raise goats, rabbits, and chickens, but also how to make soap from goat milk, and Trish had taught her how to can vegetables and make jam. On her own, she'd learned how to grow microgreens, which she sold both locally and to an exclusive buyer from Tulsa.

The farm stand, where she sold her vegetables, soaps, canned goods, and jams, probably looked like nothing more than a large wooden shed from where she and Christopher stood. But what Chris obviously didn't realize was just how much traffic the farmer's market generated. She often sold out before the end of the day and was able to keep enough produce and products stocked and growing to open up the market even in the winter.

He'd know soon enough though, as would his sister if she ever ventured out of the house long enough to see Shea in action. Saturday was the busiest day at the farmer's market. If the twins paid close enough attention, they'd see that many of the little stands pulled in thousands of dollars on a single Saturday.

"There's nothing to do here," Carrie announced with a melodramatic sigh, folding her arms when she came outside to join them.

Shea turned and smiled, shaking her head. At twenty, the twins were in their third year of college, and she had hoped that they'd each be developing their visions for the future.

But so far, it looked as though college for her daughter had merely been an extension of her high school years. She seemed to be much more interested in scrolling through social media than she was in speaking with her mother or brother, and Shea had to admit that she was more than a bit worried about it.

"We go to school in the middle of Missouri, Carrie," Chris said dryly. "It's not like central Oklahoma is all that different."

"Columbia is nothing like it is here," Carrie said, giving him a look. "There's at least some culture there."

"You'd be surprised what you can find to do around here," Shea replied, working hard to keep her tone light and to not take Carrie's comments personally.

"Knock it off, Carrie," Chris warned, glaring at his sister.

The twins typically got along so well. Shea wondered if there had been a larger conversation between them that hadn't gone well.

"Hey, how about we take a trip into town for lunch?" she asked.

"And eat what? A triple decker heart attack burger?" Carrie muttered.

"Sis, stop," Chris said, shooting his mom an apologetic look.

"No, actually, one of my best customers runs a farm to table bistro called Farm to Fork," Shea replied, choosing to overlook Carrie's rudeness...for now. "The food is amazing and everything is made from local produce."

Carrie raised an eyebrow and stuffed her hands into the pocket of her jeans. "You have a farm to table restaurant in this backwater place?"

"Okay, you just need to stop," Christopher said calmly, his voice like steel.

"It's alright, Chris," Shea said with a rueful smile.

She'd prepared herself to weather the storm when the kids came to visit. The last time she'd seen them before they went off to college, she'd been drowning in the depths of misery that had descended upon her when her husband left town with everything they had.

It had been tough to put on a happy face when she felt like she was dying inside, but Shea had tried. She'd made her whole life about the kids, putting her own needs to the side and crying after they were in bed at night, or in the shower, so that she wouldn't inflict her pain on them. She thought she'd done a pretty good job of being there for them, but the time flew by in such a whirlwind that it was hard to know. Until now.

"Look, we all need food, so let's just give it a shot. We'll go have lunch in town," Shea said gently. "Maybe it'll be a bit easier to understand my choice once you see a little bit of what life is like around here."

She had introduced them to Trish's family, and wanted to have a get-together, but Trish wisely suggested that it might be better for the twins to see more of their mother's life before distracting them with the whole Demarcus family, and all of their associated noise and hubbub.

"Something else I've considered," Shea had confided in her best friend the night before the twins were scheduled to arrive. "I wonder if the kids realize that when they leave school, if they need a soft place to land in between semesters, this is it."

"What do you mean, 'this is it?'" Trish had asked, looking puzzled.

"Just that their dad is in federal prison, maybe for the rest of his life," Shea said. "And the life they're used to looks nothing like the life I have here."

"Yeah, there definitely might be an interesting adjustment period," Trish had agreed. "You managed to fit in and do whatever needed to be done shortly after you first arrived, but you chose this. They didn't."

Shea kept the thought to herself after telling Trish and observed the twins' reactions when they came to the farm. Carrie's face, as she'd studied the stylishly rustic interior of the farmhouse, had a look on it like she had suddenly found herself on another planet, where the aliens just might be hostile. Then, when they ventured outside and neared the goat pen and chicken coop, her expression had changed from mildly disturbed to utterly disgusted.

"What is that awful smell?" she had blurted, holding a hand over her nose and mouth while they walked around the yard for the initial tour.

"This is a farm, Carrie," Chris had said, rolling his eyes at his sister's antics.

Shea hadn't taken anything her daughter had said to heart, the twins had probably felt understandably abandoned when their father left the country without a word and their mother had been barred from even walking into their repossessed home. They'd had no idea what had happened between their mom and dad – Shea had spared them that – but she often wondered if they thought that the divorce had been her fault. In her resolve to be fair to her ex, had she cast herself in the role of bad guy in her kids' eyes?

She grabbed her purse after running upstairs to wash her hands, brush her teeth, and put on a fresh blouse. "Ready for lunch?" she asked, coming back down the stairs refreshed and with a brave smile.

Chris nodded and grabbed her keys from the basket on the foyer table. Carrie let out another exaggerated sigh and headed for the Jeep without a word. She opened the back door and flopped into the seat, slumping down, arms crossed.

Chris handed over the keys as they left the house. "Do you want to drive?" Shea asked. "I'll tell you where to go."

"Yeah, that'd be great." He nodded, looking as though he was trying to smile and couldn't quite make it.

Following Shea's directions, he headed down the driveway, passing the farm stands and turned left onto the highway toward town. "I can't believe that's where you work," Carrie said as they passed the stands.

Shea chuckled. "That's the easiest part of the job," she replied. "The real work takes place long before the stand opens up for the farmer's market."

Carrie didn't bother to respond and stayed quiet for the rest of the ride into town. Shea directed Chris as he drove to the restaurant. The parking lot was teeming with cars, trucks, and even a handful of four wheelers when they arrived.

"It seems popular at least," Carrie commented when Chris pulled into a parking space.

"The food really is excellent," Shea replied. "I think you'll like it."

Again, no response from Carrie. Shea shook it off and led them inside, hoping her daughter might loosen up a bit once she relaxed and tasted the incredible food.

"Hi, welcome in," one of the servers greeted Shea when she walked in with the twins behind her.

"Would you like a table in the corner or a booth up front?" she asked, grabbing menus.

"Table," Carrie answered before Shea could reply.

"Sure thing, follow me," the server said, heading toward the far end of the large dining room. She set the menus down at each place and assured them that someone would be with them soon. Chris pulled a chair out for his mother. Shea's heart felt like it would burst with joy at his small act of kindness. Carrie settled herself into a chair, picked up her menu and opened it. Her expression, which had been sour since before they even left the farm, improved dramatically as she scanned the selections inside the menu. Her eyebrows rose and her eyes widened as she read.

"Impressed yet?" Shea asked, bracing herself for a prickly reply.

"I'm surprised by the choices, but let's wait and see how good the food actually is. I mean, it could just be a case of false advertising," Carrie replied, sounding far less certain than she had before.

"Who do you have with you today, Shea?" Dylan Branch asked, approaching their table.

"These are my twins, Chris and Carrie," Shea replied. "Guys, this is Dylan Branch, owner of Farm to Fork."

Chris stood slightly out of his chair and held out his hand. Dylan hesitated for a moment, then shook it.

"Nice to meet you," Chris said, ever the perfect gentleman. "Mom says you buy a lot of vegetables from her."

Dylan nodded. Shea held her breath, wondering how the typically cranky restaurateur would respond.

"I purchase all of my ingredients from the farmer's market on your mother's farm, and most of them are from her gardens," Dylan said, nodding. "Believe it or not, your mother has learned the market faster than just about anyone I've ever seen in my life."

Shea saw Carrie look up from her menu when she heard Dylan's kudos.

"I'll admit I've been trying hard to wrap my head around how she could possibly make a living growing and selling vegetables," Chris admitted.

Dylan chuckled. "Trust me, she knows how to price things high enough to pay her bills and keep me behind on mine," he said.

"Gee, thanks, Dylan." Shea smiled and shook her head. "My kids are going to think I'm some sort of ruthless farm stand tycoon."

"You're quite welcome. In fact, you can make it up to me by adding me to your list of microgreens customers." Dylan smirked. "Go ahead and put me at the top of your list and lower the price by twenty percent while you're at it."

"I can only do one of those things for you, Dylan," Shea said, affecting an innocent look. "I'll just let you guess which one."

Dylan rolled his eyes. "Nice meetin' y'all." He nodded to the kids, before heading back to the kitchen.

"I can't believe how good that food was, Mom," Carrie exclaimed from the back seat on their way home. "I honestly didn't expect to find such a progressive place out here in the middle of nowhere."

"Progressive?" Shea repeated. "What do you mean?"

"Locally sourced. Mostly organic. Vegan options… you know," Carrie said, waving a hand breezily.

"Carrie is on this food shaming kick," Chris replied, making a face. "It's because she hangs out with the food snobs at school."

"Oh, food snobs sound like fun," Shea said. "Would I like these people?"

"They wouldn't like you," Carrie snickered. "Particularly since you exploit your poor animals for profit the way you do."

"Carrie Michelle," Chris growled, glaring at his sister in the rearview mirror.

"Exploit? Really? It doesn't seem like you mind the 'exploitation' too much when your tuition is paid every month," Shea said quietly, not bothering to turn around.

Carrie was silent, and when Shea took a quick glance in the rearview mirror, the high color in her daughter's cheeks and her sullen expression as she gazed out of the window at the Oklahoma countryside passing by, told her that she might have just ruined the twins' entire visit.

CHAPTER TWO

Clarence the Rooster bellowed his good morning call just after five the next morning. Shea tossed back the covers and put the heels of her hands over her eyes. Her sleep had been spotty at best. Carrie and Chris had gone to bed without saying much and Shea thought she had overheard Carrie tell her brother that she couldn't wait for the week to be over and done with.

She dressed as noiselessly as she could and headed outside. Carrie and Chris had each taken a spare bedroom, and as she snuck by their doors, trying not to disturb them, Shea considered what life might be like if they had to come home to stay for a while after graduation. She knew that she should want that to happen but given their reluctance to even stay for a week, she sincerely hoped that it wouldn't. If the three of them were going to have a good relationship, it looked like they'd be better off living apart.

"Good morning, Annabelle," she said when she entered the pen with the goats.

Annabelle had joined the herd as a baby and had just given birth for the first time. Milking her was part of Shea's regular morning routine, along with the one other nanny goat in the pen. When she was finished, she lugged two full pails of milk to the garden shed and placed them in the fridge, before heading to the chicken coop to check for eggs and feed the chickens.

Chris stood in her path when she emerged from the coop.

"Good morning," she greeted him with a smile, genuinely glad to see him. As far as she knew, he would at least speak to her.

"Morning, Mom," he replied.

She noticed that his shirt was inside out, and his shoes were untied.

"You're up early," Shea said, deciding not to mention his somewhat hilarious appearance. He might not appreciate her sense of humor. "You know you can sleep until noon, and I won't say a word to you, right?"

"I know." Chris smiled. "I want to see what the farmers market is like. Do you need any help? I see that you did whatever it is that you do for the chickens, so what's next?" he asked.

Shea's heart leapt. Her son was actually interested. "Well, next I'll head to the garden to pick the vegetables that are ready for today and then I'm off to the greenhouse to do the same thing."

"Can I tag along?" Chris asked.

Shea grinned so widely that she was surprised her teeth didn't dry out. "Of course you can, I'd be glad to have company. I'm sort of shocked that you want to tag along, but I'd love to show you what I do every day."

Chris stayed at her side when she ventured into the zucchini patch, taking care not to step on the plants. She pointed out the large, green zucchinis resting on the ground and demonstrated how to pick them by holding onto the vine and twisting each one carefully to prevent damage to the plant. Once they were done there, they moved on, selecting only the best and ripest summer squashes, butternut squashes, and cucumbers.

"I can't believe you pick all of these vegetables every day," Chris commented when they made it to the end of the first row.

"Oh, this is just the beginning," Shea replied. "We still have to make our way through the carrots, tomatoes, peppers, green beans, and peas. And that's before we even get to the greenhouses."

Chris was a trooper, following his mother and helping as best as he could with the morning chores. He looked positively astonished at the sheer volume of produce when she finally filled the last wooden crate and placed it on her flatbed trailer. Afterward, she carefully stacked the cartons of eggs on top and headed to check the tractor hitch.

"I can see why you drive the tractor down there," Chris remarked.

"It's so much easier. I don't know what I'd do without it. If I had to hand carry everything down like I did in the beginning, the market would be over for the day by the time I finished," Shea said, chuckling. "Do you want to try it?"

"Try what?" he asked, brows raised.

"Driving the tractor, of course," Shea replied. "Just down to the end of the driveway."

"I don't know, Mom." Chris gazed at the tractor as if it might bite. "I'm not exactly familiar with farm equipment."

"Can you drive a stick shift?" Shea persisted.

Chris nodded. "Yeah, I mean, I have," he said. "I mean, like, in driver's training, remember? We had to learn that to pass."

"Yeah, I remember," Shea said. "I was glad that your driving instructor was such a laid-back guy. But, no worries, this is an older tractor," she explained. "If you can handle a five speed, you can handle this. I promise it isn't hard. I learned in one lesson."

"Who taught you?" Chris asked, one eyebrow raised.

"Trish's husband Barry came over one day and showed me how. A couple of their kids help me out on the farm from time to time and both of them know how to drive the tractor too."

Chris stared at her for a moment, a sweet smile on his face. "That's pretty great that you have friends like that here."

"Yeah, it really is," Shea agreed. "Now climb on up in the cab. I'll sit beside you and coach you along the way."

"If you say so," he said, climbing up into the driver's seat. He seemed uncertain, but he was definitely being a good sport about the whole thing.

Shea gave him a quick rundown of the controls and waited while he turned the motor over. Once he started it up, Shea nodded, and he put the tractor into gear. Moving cautiously, he got it turned around and headed slowly toward the end of the driveway.

"What do I do once I get there?" he asked, darting a glance at the farm stand. "We didn't cover that part."

"Slow it down by dropping a gear and pull to a stop behind the first stand on the right, just like you would with a car. It's the largest one there." She pointed. They practically glided to a stop as Chris put the tractor in a perfect position for unloading. Once he turned off the engine, Shea reached over and shook his shoulder. "Way to go! You're like a real farm guy already – I'm so impressed," she said with a huge grin.

"Thanks, Mom." Chris smiled, a hint of blush rising in his cheeks. Apparently, he took a compliment about as well as his mother. He jumped down from the tractor and began asking questions about where to put the wooden crates filled with freshly picked vegetables. The two of them worked side by side, unloading the crates and filling bins like they'd been a team all along.

Shortly after they opened up the front windows of the stand, Shea saw Carrie sauntering down the driveway toward them.

"Wow, what a good little son you are, helping Mom on the farm," she said with a smirk as she leaned against the door frame of the stand.

"I'm just learning about her life, Carrie," Chris said quietly. "Just back off."

"What? Maybe I wanted to come down here, too," Carrie said.

"Really? Were you planning on helping? Or having a nice conversation? Or are you just going to continue being an absolute jerk?" Chris whispered. "Because let me tell you, this is hard work. Mom does more than you realize."

"Seriously?" Carrie looked skeptical.

"Seriously," Chris said, shooting her a look that seemed as though he was daring her to say something.

Shea pretended that she hadn't heard their conversation. "Do you want some coffee, hon?" she asked Carrie. "I can make it hot or iced."

A corner of her daughter's mouth tilted upward in what was almost a smile. "Iced coffee sounds good," she said.

"Hey, Mom," Chris said when Shea turned on the coffee maker. "I think someone is coming."

Shea leaned out of one of the front windows and glanced to the left, then waved when she saw her bestie's SUV slip into a parking spot, saying a silent thanks for reinforcements. "That's Trish," she said. "The farm stand next to mine is hers. She'll want iced coffee, too, so I'll make yours first, Carrie."

"Thanks, Mom," the young woman replied quietly. Shea hadn't yet detected any signs of leftover resentment after their rather unpleasant interaction the day before. So far, so good.

"Good morning, Beaumont Family," Trish sang out, her Oklahoma drawl seeming exaggerated when she approached the farm stand. She carried a covered dish in her hands. "I brought y'all some fresh cinnamon rolls. They're still nice and warm. Hello again, twins, I've heard so much about the two of you," Trish said warmly. "But I'm hoping to get more of a chance to chat at some point."

"That would be nice, ma'am," Chris replied politely.

"Are those gluten free?" Carrie asked, lifting the lid and peering down at the cinnamon rolls after Trish set them on the counter.

"Carrie," Chris hissed, under his breath.

"Actually, no," Trish said, her smile faltering only slightly. "But I do have some baked apples in my truck. Would you like one?"

Embarrassed by Carrie's lack of manners, Shea was grateful for Trish's class and compassion.

"I'd love one, thanks," Carrie said, shocking Shea by actually smiling at Trish. "I'm sorry if that sounded bad. I'm just kind of cranky in the morning before I have coffee."

"No worries," Trish replied. "Do you want to follow me back to my truck? I can give you a nice warm apple to sink your teeth into, and I have it on good authority that they go well with coffee."

"Sure, that'd be great," Carrie said, following Trish out of the farm stand.

As soon as they left, Chris rested his arm on his mother's shoulder. "It's so hard to be patient with her sometimes," he said, sighing. "But it'll pay off in the long run."

"Very mature words," Shea said, putting her arm around his waist and giving him a squeeze.

Chris shrugged. "I took a psych class last year, and then I started volunteering at an at-risk youth shelter. Carries started hanging out with the Cause of the Month Club."

"What on earth is the Cause of the Month Club? Is that a real thing?" Shea asked.

Chris laughed. "No. It's just the nature of the group of students that Carrie hangs out with," he replied. "She met them at the end of our freshman year. Their favorite pastime is finding injustices in the world and trying to help eliminate them. But it seems like they're only committed to a cause if it involves something that affects them directly."

"Really? Like what?" Shea asked, fascinated by this glimpse into the twins' relationship and college life.

"Like, they wanted to boycott a certain manufacturer because of some legal maneuvering they'd done to stop workers from getting raises, but then they found out that the manufacturer produced their favorite boba tea, so they moved on to something else," Chris said, rolling his eyes.

Shea stifled her amusement when she saw Carrie approaching with her baked apple.

"This is amazing," she said, savoring a bite. "It's seriously yummy."

"Good," Shea replied. "And just in time…your coffee is ready." She handed Carrie her iced coffee.

"Thank you, I need it." Carrie actually smiled and Shea practically wilted with relief. The last thing she had wanted was to drive a wedge between them.

Trish returned to the stand and served up cinnamon rolls for herself, Shea, and Chris, then, balancing a paper plate with her cinnamon roll and the iced coffee that Shea handed over, she headed back to her own farm stand.

"I like your friend," Carrie said. "But does she really have like six kids?"

Shea grinned. "Yep, she really does, and she fosters kids from time to time too." She left Carrie wide-eyed and headed to the counter in the back to package the tomatoes and smaller cucumbers into pint baskets.

"What can I do to help?" Chris asked, peering over her shoulder.

Shea continued packing vegetable while she answered. "Well, you can put these baskets in the fridge," she suggested. "I need to put a few more of the things in jars out as well."

"I can do that," Carrie said, astonishing her mother. Fortunately, Shea's back was turned so it was easier to hide her reaction. "Where are they?"

"They're on the shelves next to the fridge. I sell a lot of cinnamon pickles, bread and butter pickles, and soy candles."

"Gotcha," Carrie replied, going to the shelves. "I'll grab some and arrange them for you."

Shea felt a bit ashamed when she wondered if Carrie's sudden personality change was because she was up to something. She spotted Helen Porter across the road at her small stand. The older woman waved, and Shea waved back, wondering what on earth was going on. First her daughter had become nicer, and now Helen, who was typically an abrasive woman, was greeting her. The familiar crunch of the gravel by her farm stand announced the first customers of the day, interrupting her thoughts.

By nine o'clock Shea had completely sold out of eggs and cucumbers. Chris had become her shadow, and a very helpful shadow at that. As soon as a customer requested something that wasn't stocked in the bins in the front of the stand, he'd grab it for her. Carrie stood back a bit and observed, jumping in whenever anyone requested goat milk soaps or candles.

"I can't believe how many people drive all the way out here for this stuff," Chris said during a lull between customers. "It's like a county fair all day long. And you said that you're open on other days of the week, too?"

Shea nodded. "I'm never open on a Sunday, because I need at least one day off. Wednesdays and Saturdays are the full farmer's market days during the season. But I also open up during the rest of the week during the growing season, too."

"What about those people from Tulsa you told us about?" Carrie asked.

Shea turned to her daughter, delighted that she had actually remembered something she'd told her about the farm stand. "For the microgreens? They come on Tuesdays and pick up as many trays as I have available," she said. "Dylan from Farm to Fork takes the rest on the following Thursday."

"Those sell really well, then?"

"Yep, all year long," Shea replied. "And they're a huge part of what pays the bills."

"This really is a profitable business," Chris observed.

Shea opened her mouth to reply but closed it again when she saw Andrea Salt, a Pawnee County Sheriff's deputy, approach the window.

"Morning, Shea," Andrea said. "Who do we have here?" she asked, nodding toward Carrie and Chris, who were standing shoulder to shoulder in front of the fridge.

"These are my twins, Chris and Carrie," Shea replied, entirely unable to keep a touch of pride from her tone. "Chris, Carrie, this is Deputy Salt."

"Andrea," she corrected with a smile, extending her hand across the counter first to Chris, then to Carrie. "Y'all are here on break from Mizzou, right?"

Chris smiled and nodded. "Yep, absolutely. Are you an alum?"

Andrea shook her head. "I'm not, but my brother went to the University of Missouri," she said. "I still cheer on the Tigers during football season."

"Did you need something, Andrea?" Shea asked with a smile.

Sheriff Seth Grayson appeared next to her at the counter before the deputy could reply. He nodded at

Shea and smiled at the kids. Shea quickly introduced Seth but left out the fact that they were dating.

"Actually, we need to speak with the three of you," Andrea said after introductions had been completed.

Shea noted that Seth didn't seem to be quite his usual self and her stomach did a worried flip flop. "What's going on?" she asked, casting a quick glance past them to see if there were any customers approaching.

"Can we step inside with you for a moment?" Andrea asked. "I'm not sure that we want word to get out just yet."

"About what?" Chris asked.

"Come on into the stand," Shea said, opening the side door and stepping out of the way. Despite the size of the farm stand compared to the others close by, five people inside seemed like a bit of a crowd.

"Where did y'all eat lunch yesterday?" Andrea asked quietly when they were all inside, with the door shut behind them.

"At Farm to Fork," Shea replied, frowning. She looked from Andrea to Seth and back again. "Why? What's going on?"

"Did you happen to see Dylan's niece, McKenna, while you were there?" Seth asked.

Shea nodded. "I think I remember seeing that she was there," she said. "We definitely saw Dylan, though. He was up to his usual friendliness."

"Did he seem…off in any way, or was there anyone there who seemed out of place?"

Shea shook her head. "No, nothing seemed off," she turned to the twins. "Did you two notice anything?"

"Nothing I remember," Carrie said with a shrug.

"Not a thing," Chris agreed.

Andrea sighed deeply. "Dylan Branch was found this morning in the kitchen by one of his staff members," she said. "Someone had taken one of his kitchen knives and…" Andrea looked down, her sentence trailing away.

"Dylan was murdered, Shea," Seth said grimly.

"What?" Shea gasped, her eyes going wide.

CHAPTER THREE

Shea sat down hard on the stool she kept in the back of the shed. She had just seen Dylan...and now he was gone. Andrea stayed where she was, but Seth moved forward to place a hand on her arm and give it a supportive squeeze. "We're all pretty stunned," he said quietly.

"It'll be a shock to the entire community," Andrea added. Seth nodded, and with a sympathetic look toward Shea, stepped back to stand beside the deputy.

"If no one saw anything out of the ordinary, I suppose our work here is done, Deputy Salt," he said, all business now.

"Thanks for letting us know," Shea murmured.

"If you happen to remember anything or think of anything you might have seen, please give me a holler," Andrea said. "Also, because I know who I'm talking to, I'm going to caution you right here and now that you need to think twice and be very careful about trying to take matters into your own hands," she warned.

"I second that, Shea," Seth said, giving her a direct look. "We have no idea what we might be dealing with here, so let's leave the sleuthing to the professionals this time."

Shea nodded numbly and turned back to the front window where a small crowd of new customers had gathered. A full half hour passed before the crowd thinned enough for a conversation with the twins, but Trish appeared in the doorway before she could say anything to them.

"Hey girl, I heard a rumor that something…bad happened to Dylan last night," Trish said. "Is it true? Is that why they were here?" she asked.

"I'm afraid so," Shea replied. "That's why they came to talk to us. We had lunch at Farm to Fork yesterday."

"So, they were asking you if you had seen anything," Trish said.

"Yeah, that's pretty much it," Shea replied.

"They did ask us about someone named McKenna," Carrie said. "I wonder if that means that she's a suspect."

"It wouldn't surprise me in the least," Trish said with a grimace. "Remember when he was a suspect in another case - she and her mom Ellen took over the bistro?"

"Another case?" Carrie said, eyebrows raised. "This is intriguing."

"There was an incident a while back and he was a suspect," Shea said, waving a hand dismissively. "But they were way off base, and I guess none of that matters now. I can't believe Dylan Branch is gone."

"I know. It's crazy to even think about," Trish said, shaking her head. "You know, I believe this calls for closing down for the day out of respect."

Shea nodded. "Yeah. I was thinking the same thing," she said. "Of course it's up to Helen and the others what they want to do, but I think we're finished here for now."

"I'll spread the word," Trish volunteered. "I'm just about sold out today anyway." She gave Shea a hug before heading back to her farm stand.

"What do we need to do to close down?" Chris asked.

Shea folded her arms over her middle and glanced about, clearly trying to focus on her tasks. "Um, we need to get all of the veggies out of the bins in the front and put them in the fridge," she replied. "If we don't have enough room, we can take them to the garden shed fridge."

"What about the candles and the other jars?" Carrie asked.

"I just like to put them back on the shelf so they'll stay cool," Shea directed.

Between the three of them, after just under ten minutes, she waved goodbye to Trish and headed for the tractor.

"Do you want me to drive back?" Chris asked.

"Sure," Shea said absently. "Why don't you climb up in the cab with your brother, Carrie? I'll walk back on my own."

"We can all fit, Mom," Carrie said gently. She took Shea's hand and walked with her to the tractor. Shea rode in silence, while Chris drove the tractor like a pro, with no instruction from his mom. He pulled it into its space behind the garden shed and cut the engine, then got out and disconnected the flatbed without having to be asked.

Shea began unloading the extra vegetables from the wagon and carrying them into the garden shed, with Carrie and Chris pitching in like they'd been doing it all their lives. Had she not been so shocked by the announcement of Dylan's death, she would have taken more time to appreciate their quiet compassion.

"I'll make us something for lunch," she announced, walking slowly toward the house. She carried a selection of vegetables along with her, though she had no idea what she was going to do with them. Staying busy seemed like a good plan for the moment.

Once inside, in the comfort of her large, homey kitchen, Shea set out her favorite medium sized pan and filled it with the right amount of water and the sugar to make lemonade, then set the pan over medium heat and turned her attention back to the veggies on her counter.

Her thoughts immediately went to the last meal she had eaten at Farm to Fork, and the interaction she had had with Dylan. The fact that someone had murdered him in the kitchen of his beloved bistro shook her to her core.

Shea began mindlessly slicing up cucumbers and onions, putting them in a large bowl as she went. She added water, sugar, and vinegar to the bowl along with salt, pepper, and spices and set it in the fridge to chill, then turned her attention back to the simple syrup that was now boiling on the stove. She took the mixture off the burner and added lemon juice for her fresh lemonade.

She decided to sauté the squash and zucchini she'd brought in to make a quick veggie sand-wich. Mixing a pint of cherry tomatoes into a caprese salad that she had been marinating in the fridge, she sliced up a loaf of homemade tomato basil bread and set everything out on the kitchen island.

After pouring the lemonade mixture into a pitcher of ice, Shea went to the kitchen door, called out to the twins, and waited for them to come inside.

By the time she heard the door open, Shea had been able to pull her thoughts together a bit. The twins would only be with her for a few more days. The last thing she wanted was to squander that precious time with them. Who knew when they might return?

"Wow, something smells amazing in here," Chris said, inhaling appreciatively. He picked up a plate and spooned a heap of the caprese salad onto it. "They make this same salad at this little Italian place in the middle of Columbia. I can't get enough of it."

"What's this bread, Mom?" Carrie asked. Shea winced. She'd forgotten about her daughter's avoidance to gluten.

"I'm sorry, honey, it's regular bread, so it has gluten," Shea replied. "I didn't know you were eating gluten-free or I would have made a different kind."

"She just started that," Chris said, helping himself to two slices of the thick, crusty bread.

"It's not medical or anything." Carrie shrugged. "I just started on it. I don't have celiac disease. I can have some." She pulled off a small piece and popped it into her mouth.

"What do you think?" Shea asked, bracing herself.

"I think gluten is awfully tasty in this case," Carrie said with a sheepish grin. She took another bite and chewed thoughtfully. "It's so tomatoey. Did these tomatoes come from your garden?"

"From last year's crop." Shea nodded. "They were sun dried and stored away over the winter. I'm not an expert baker, but I added double the tomatoes the recipe calls for and used some of the basil from my herb garden. I don't sell herbs though; those are just for my use."

"It's so good," Carrie said, her words muffled by a mouth full of the bread. "I can't imagine being able to eat like this all of the time."

Shea laughed and handed her a glass of fresh squeezed lemonade. "This isn't sugar free or low carb, either," she warned.

"You look like you've lost weight, Mom," Carrie commented, after washing her bite of bread down with a swig of lemonade. "At least from the last time I saw you."

"Thanks. I'm probably just in better shape from all of the exercise I get from running this place."

"And all the vegetables you eat," Carrie replied.

Shea fought the urge to run around the counter and trap her daughter in a bear hug. Conversation and laughter hadn't come so easily for the two of them since the twins were preteens. But she resisted. The last thing she wanted was for the moment to turn awkward or for the sweet spell to somehow be broken.

"So, Mom," Chris said when they were all gathered around the table with their lunch. "What's with you and the sheriff?"

Shea felt the heat rise in her cheeks as she desperately tried to think of an answer. She pushed a tomato around on her plate for a moment while she gathered her thoughts.

"Who cares, Chris?" Carrie came to her rescue. "Mom and Dad were divorced before we even left for school and Dad is in prison."

Shea held her breath. It was the first reference to their father and his prison sentence since they'd arrived.

"I was just asking," Chris said, arching an eyebrow at his sister, then turned back to Shea. "Are you dating him?"

Shea nodded, hoping her blush wasn't as profound as it felt. "Yes, I am. We met two years ago, shortly after I moved in here, and became friends. We just started dating not too long ago."

"Is it serious, do you think? Am I about to have a sheriff for a stepfather?" Chris persisted.

"Oh please," Shea said, chuckling. "No one is getting married around here, unless one of you has an announcement to make."

"Nope, not me," Carrie said, holding up her hands.

"Definitely not me." Chris laughed. "I get the point. I was just wondering."

"He's a nice guy," Shea said. "He is a good man, really. He treats me well."

"What did they mean when they said something about getting to the bottom of things, or whatever?" Carrie asked. "I thought that was kind of an odd thing for them to say to you. Was that because of your relationship with the sheriff?"

Shea covered her face with her hands and shook her head. "Not exactly," she said. "But, for you to understand why that was said, you need to know a little about what I've been through for the past couple of years."

"Wow," Chris said. "That's not too ominous or anything," he commented dryly.

Over the next half hour or so, Shea gave them the highlights of her adventures since arriving in her new Oklahoma home. While she told them about how she had helped crack major criminal cases, she left out any of the details that might have made them worry about her.

"So, let me get this straight," Chris said, seeming deep in thought as he paced around the room. Shea noted how very much he looked like his father at that moment. "You've become some sort of a detective since you moved here?"

Shea chuckled. "I wouldn't say that," she replied. "I've just gone digging for answers and managed to figure out a few things, that's all."

"It sounds like you've figured out quite a few things," Carrie commented. "Were you involved with Dad's case too?"

"It's more like I was pulled into that," Shea said carefully. "His old business partner was found dead not far from here. And then your dad showed up here, too. It really was all a matter of timing. But I can assure you that I didn't try to get your dad put away."

Chris nodded. "I think we already knew that, but it's still nice to hear it from you," he said.

"All I know is that you've changed quite a bit, Mom," Carrie said. "And I think you should ignore what they said."

"Huh? Ignore what, exactly?" Shea asked.

"What the deputy and your boyfriend said."

Shea felt the heat beginning to creep up from the base of her neck and onto her cheeks when Carrie mentioned the word boyfriend. "Oh? So, you think I ought to look into who killed Dylan Branch?"

"He was your friend, wasn't he?" Carrie asked.

"More like 'frenemy,' but yes, I did care about him," Shea said, smiling ruefully.

"Do you think this McKenna person could have killed him?" Chris asked.

"No way," Shea replied, shaking her head. "She's not necessarily my favorite person, for a variety of reasons, but I don't think for a moment that she would have murdered her uncle."

"What are we waiting for, then?" Carrie asked, a sparkle of mischief in her eyes. "Let's figure out who did."

CHAPTER FOUR

"I think we should go to town and have a look around," Carrie suggested, once they were finished with lunch. She put the dishes in the sink, while Chris wiped down the table and Shea put the food away.

"You want to drive around in town?" Shea asked. "How would that help? What would we be looking for?"

Carrie shrugged. "I have no idea," she replied. "You're the detective. You tell me what we should be looking for."

"I'm not even close to being a detective," Shea protested, chuckling.

"Okay, fine, whatever…amateur sleuth then, if that makes you feel better. That's what they call people who look into murders and stuff in the books I like to read."

"I don't think I could even be classified as that, but if I want to look into things, I would usually start online," Shea said.

"Online? Why would you start online?" Chris asked.

"Well, because there isn't much I can do anywhere else," Shea replied. "Farm to Fork is going to be closed down for a while, I would guess. It's not like they're going to let us go inside and check the crime scene out."

"Yeah, that makes sense. Okay, what would you look for online?"

"I would start out looking at Dylan's social media profiles and activity, just to see if there's been anyone who might be upset with him, or anything odd that might stand out," Shea said. "I'm really curious as to what I might find if I take a look at McKenna Lambert's social media as well."

"That's Dylan's niece's name?"

"Yep. She and her mother Ellen had a falling out with Dylan back when I first came here."

"That's when he was suspected of murder?" Chris clarified.

"Yeah. It seems like so long ago. They took over the bistro for a little while he was being held pending investigation," Shea replied.

"Mom, it sounds to me like you should probably consider the fact that McKenna and her mother might still feel like they had an ax to grind with Dylan," Carrie said.

"I mean, obviously, there's a very good reason why the sheriff and Deputy Salt asked us about her," Shea said slowly, thinking. "But there may be another angle to this. McKenna is many things, but I don't think dumb is one of them. She would have to know that if something happened to Dylan, everyone would be looking in her direction and her mother's. I think, since we don't have any actual information about what happened, or why, we should start by looking for anyone aside from McKenna or her mother who might have a reason to harm him."

"Is it possible he might have upset someone connected with his business?" Chris asked.

Shea smiled sadly and nodded. "Yeah, it's distinctly possible. Dylan was a very *colorful* human being – opinionated and as outspoken as the day is long. He definitely had a way of upsetting the people around him, including me when we first met."

"Well, you have an alibi, at least," Carrie pointed out reasonably. "You were here with us all night."

"Well, I guess that's at least one detail we won't have to worry about," Shea replied. "I think we also need to consider that maybe Dylan wasn't the target. It might have been another one of his cooks or a staff member, or McKenna, or someone else."

"Maybe it was just a simple case of an interrupted robbery," Chris mused.

"We need to make a list," Carrie said. "I need some-thing to write with and something to write on, please."

"I agree. I'll be right back." Shea stood and headed down the main hall to her office. She unplugged her laptop and picked up a couple of pens and an empty notebook. As sad as she was about Dylan's untimely passing, the fact that the twins were so invested in helping her to figure out what happened made her glow a little bit. She'd wondered how to keep her relationship with them growing and would never have dreamed that joining forces to solve a crime would be in their future.

"So, what do we do first?" Carrie asked Shea when she returned and handed over the pens and notebook.

"First we need to make a list of all of the people who might have had a disagreement of some kind with Dylan," Shea replied.

"Maybe you should write down the name of the niece first," Chris suggested.

"McKenna Lambert," Shea reminded her. "And her mother's name is Ellen DuBois."

"What relation is Ellen to Dylan?" Carrie asked.

"Ellen is Dylan's sister, but she's much older," Shea said. "When he was in jail a couple of years ago, she was more than eager to step in and try to take the bistro from him."

"Yeah, that sounds like something a loving older sister would do," Chris said dryly, shaking his head.

"Yeah, she's a real peach," Shea agreed.

"Do you think she is capable of killing her own brother though?" Carrie asked, busily taking notes.

Shea sat down and opened her laptop. "That's hard to say. I really don't know enough about her to say for sure."

"So Ellen is definitely on the suspect list then," Carrie said.

"We don't know for sure," Chris cautioned his sister. "We have no idea where she was when he was killed. For all we know, she might have been on vacation in Florida."

"Exactly. Anything is possible, and we need to do some checking before making determinations," Shea agreed. "That's where social media can help out."

Samson, Shea's beloved golden retriever, interrupted their workflow temporarily by entering the room and insisting upon receiving love and attention from each member of the family before heading to the special rug that stayed in front of the fireplace for him even in the middle of summer. He turned his required three circles before slumping down onto the rug in a fluffy golden heap.

"I can't believe you actually got a dog, Mom," Chris said, grinning. He got up, went to the fireplace and sat on the floor next to Samson. Never one to miss a golden opportunity, Samson shifted closer and rested his head in Chris's lap. "What a good boy," Chris murmured to the dog, stroking his silky ears.

"Where did you get him?" Carrie asked. She got out of her chair and sat on the end of the couch closest to Chris and a very contented Samson.

"I didn't get him. He kind of got me," Shea said with a fond smile. "He just sort of appeared one day and has followed me everywhere I go ever since. You should have seen how filthy he was when I first met him. I had no idea he was a golden retriever – he just looked like a scruffy brown dog."

"He just showed up here on the farm?" Chris asked, surprised.

"Yes, he did. It was like he knew he was supposed to be here. I took him to the vet in town and she said he was healthy," Shea replied. "We put out a notice for anyone missing a golden retriever and never heard a thing, so he just stayed." She chuckled.

"So he became ours," Carrie said, sliding down from her seat on the couch to sit next to him. She stroked his side and informed him that he was indeed the very best boy.

"Ours?" Chris said, a smile playing about his lips. "I think Samson is Mom's dog."

"He can totally be ours," Shea said quickly. "I mean, you guys might have a different opinion, but as far as I am concerned, this is our house. Our farm. Our home."

"I guess we really don't have anywhere else to call home anymore," Carrie said, her tone seeming more resigned than bitter.

"You could still go back to Flagstaff, if you feel like that's home to you," Shea said gently. "I think that would be a perfectly normal thing for you to do if you'd like. Just because your dad and I aren't there doesn't mean that it can't feel like home to you two. It just isn't home for me anymore."

Carrie shrugged. "I went back last summer," she said. "Just to visit some old friends."

"And how was it?" Shea asked, feeling slightly hurt that this was the first time she'd heard about that particular event.

Carrie trailed her fingers through Samson's silky fur. "It wasn't the same," she said, with a faraway look on her face. "I sort of felt like an outsider. It's like everyone else moved on without me."

"Is that why you put up with those…interesting people you call friends at Mizzou?" Chris asked.

"Christopher!" Shea exclaimed, surprised.

"It's okay, Mom," Carrie replied with a sigh. "He's right. They really aren't my friends. I'm sort of looking forward to graduation next year so they can hurry up and forget I exist."

"Oh wow, I'm so sorry, honey," Shea said, her heart aching for her daughter. No wonder she'd been acting out a bit since coming to Oklahoma. Carrie shrugged and waved her hand dismissively.

Chris had rolled onto his back next to Samson, who seemed quite pleased with the extra attention. "Hey, you guys," he said, holding his cell phone in the air above his face. "I don't mean to interrupt but I think I might have just found something."

CHAPTER FIVE

"Really? Like what?" Shea asked, setting her laptop aside and leaning forward in the comfy overstuffed chair that faced the couch.

"This guy, Dylan," Chris began. "He's sort of a larger guy, right? Receding hairline?"

"We met him yesterday, Chris," Carrie said dryly.

"I know, but I don't exactly remember every specific detail. I was pretty much preoccupied with the menu," Chris replied. "It's not like I had any way of knowing that the guy was going to get murdered in his kitchen and that I might need to recall details about him."

Shea got up to kneel beside Chris and peered at the photo that he had enlarged on his phone screen. "Yep, that's him," she confirmed. "But I don't think I've ever seen that social media account before."

"Have you looked at his other social media profile?" Chris asked.

"I have, but not for some time," Shea admitted. "I had no idea he had two."

"He has this one listed under *Veggie Dude*," Chris said.

"How on earth did you find it?" Shea asked, impressed.

Chris sighed and looked as though he was weighing his words carefully. "Honestly Mom, it's too complicated to explain in a single conversation and we have more important things to focus on right now," he said. "But that's definitely his photo, right?"

"Without question." Shea nodded.

"Chris took a bunch of extra computer classes at school," Carrie explained. "He knows how to find anyone online." She grinned.

"I just know how to find profiles that are linked to a specific person. No big deal," Chris replied.

"So, what did you find out about Dylan so far?" Shea asked.

"He made a post five days ago about a company that he apparently wasn't too pleased with," Chris said. "Here, let me read it to you."

Whatever you do, don't trust the clowns at Organix Solutions. Working with them is like finding yourself in the middle of a three-ring circus.

"What's Organix Solutions?" Carrie asked.

"Looks like some sort of food distribution company," Chris replied. "But anyway, the important thing is that this account seems to be an anonymous account for Dylan. He has quite a few posts about different companies and people who have made him upset."

"He didn't post about the local farmer's market, did he?" Shea asked, bracing herself.

"Not recently as far as I can tell," Chris said, still scanning pages on his phone. "But if you've had a run in with him in the past, I wouldn't be surprised that he had something to say about it on here."

"Yikes." Shea grimaced.

Chris nodded. "Yeah, this profile is filled with his rants about businesses and individual people who have crossed him. At least in his mind. Not that I want to be the bearer of bad news, but I'm guessing that most of the people that he complained about could probably be added to the suspect list...and there are several."

"Unfortunately, I agree. We should probably pay attention to the other comments," Shea replied. "I mean, unless this was a crime of passion and opportunity, killing someone in their own business takes time to plan, so the culprit might have been someone that Dylan mentioned ages ago." She sighed.

"So, do you want me to write down Organix Solutions, or no?" Carrie asked.

"Yes, write it down," Shea said. "We should check into them first, since they were the last disagreeable entity before...the incident. I know all too well how Dylan could be when he had an issue with a vendor, or if he even just thought there was an issue. I learned that the hard way on my first day as a vendor at the farmer's market."

"This guy sounds like he wasn't exactly a wonderful human, Mom," Chris commented, scrolling through more posts on his phone.

"He was a character, for sure," Shea replied. "But beneath that gruff exterior, he was also a very good businessman, and he cared a lot about his employees and customers. Dylan could have opened multiple bistros like Farm to Fork."

"Why didn't he, then?" Carrie asked. "I mean, I've been to a lot of organic, farm to table restaurants like his and his definitely stands out. I honestly couldn't believe that you had a place like that out here in the middle of nowhere."

"You made that part clear," Chris muttered, still focused on his phone.

"What's that supposed to mean?" Carrie asked, arching an eyebrow.

"Maybe that you made it seem like Mom had moved to the worst place on the planet, Carrie," Chris said, giving his sister a pointed look. "You acted like a spoiled brat the first day we were here."

"Chris," Shea said softly. "Let's just leave that alone, alright?"

"Wow. Do you agree with him, Mom?" Carrie set the pen down and tapped her foot.

Shea sighed, wishing that Chris would've kept these particular thoughts to himself. "You were a bit negative…"

"Ya think?" Chris snorted.

Shea cast a warning glance in his direction, but it looked like he was pretending to be far too absorbed in his research to have seen her.

"…but I don't blame you," she finished. "I'm living a completely different lifestyle in a place that we'd never even been to before I made a pretty major life decision." Shea smiled, remembering. "I actually bought this place sight unseen."

"Interesting choice," Chris commented. "How did you know what to do to even survive, never mind running a whole farm?"

"The woman who sold me the property left me a long list of instructions, and I just had to jump in and do it," Shea said with a shrug.

"But why here? Why a farmer's market?" Carrie asked.

"Two reasons, really," Shea replied. "One, Oklahoma isn't that far from Missouri, so I'd be relatively close in case you two needed me or wanted to visit. And two, I wanted a piece of real estate that could be an income producer so I could make a living for myself. I did look into purchasing a duplex in Boston, but I figured that the risk was too high. The cost of living there is probably ten times more in Boston than it is here. Besides, this was the most different, off-the-wall, brave choice that I could make."

"Hey, Mom," Chris interrupted, gazing intently at his phone. "Have you ever heard of Fisher's Local?"

"Fisher's Local?" Shea frowned. "No, it doesn't ring a bell. What is it? A tavern or bar or something?"

"Nope, it's some sort of fish farm place," Chris replied. "And about six months ago our buddy Veggie Dude ranted about them in capital letters for a week straight."

"Oh boy. What kinds of things did he say?" Shea asked, sitting on the floor next to Carrie.

"Why don't you look this stuff up on Mom's laptop, Chris," Carrie suggested. "That way we can all see it at the same time."

"Hang on," Chris said, sitting up. He bear crawled over to the chair and picked up the laptop, then moved to the far end of the couch and took a seat on the floor next to Shea. The three of them sat elbow to elbow with their backs against the couch. Samson raised his head briefly, then lowered it again and closed his eyes contentedly. "Alright, let's do this," Chris said, lacing his fingers together and popping his knuckles. "Is it okay if I go into your internet browser, Mom?" he asked.

"Of course. Do whatever you need to," Shea replied. She watched, impressed, as her son's fingers flew over the keyboard. He called up the same profile he had viewed on his phone and moved backward through the posts until he found what he was looking for.

"See? Right here. He even tags Fisher's Local in his rants." Chris pointed at the screen. "He accused them of everything from selling nasty fish to fraud and overbilling."

"And if they're tagged in that, it also means that they saw it too," Shea said.

"Yep. If they check their social media, they definitely would have seen it." Chris nodded.

"That sounds like a motive for revenge if I've ever heard one," Carrie commented.

"I think we need to look into several different possibilities here," Shea mused, her mind whirling. "And we'll start tomorrow with Fisher's Local. They're only about an hour and a half from here."

"Wait…you actually want to go there," Chris asked. "Like, in person?"

Shea shrugged and smiled. "Sure. Why not? I'll get up earlier than usual to make sure that the chores get done and we should be able to leave around eight."

"I'll help," Carrie volunteered. "Just get me up, please." She grinned.

"You're going to help Mom with the farm chores?" Chris said, his mouth falling open in surprise.

"Yes. I'm perfectly capable of doing things, you know," Carrie shot back. "Besides, I think it would be fun to learn more about the animals."

CHAPTER SIX

Clarence beat Shea's alarm clock the following morning, crowing his heart out like it was his only job. At top volume, he succeeded in waking both Shea and Carrie, and in an unusual turn of events, Shea was grateful to the cantankerous rooster. Getting up earlier meant hitting the road earlier. She dressed quickly, headed downstairs, and was somewhat astonished when she found a very sleepy, but smiling Carrie standing in the middle of the kitchen with two mugs of fresh coffee.

"Yes Mom, I know how to run a coffee maker, too." She chuckled, handing Shea one of the mugs of coffee.

"I never had any doubt," Shea said, taking a sip. She decided to keep it to herself that the coffee was as weak as tap water. She'd make up for the caffeine deficiency later with a latte from her favorite place by the lake on the way to the fishery.

"What should we do first?" Carrie asked.

After a few big swigs, just to show appreciation for her daughter's effort, Shea set her mug in the sink and motioned toward the kitchen door. "First thing we do is feed and check on the animals," she replied. "I have to milk two goats and check for eggs."

"Okay, cool. Show me how to do the feeding, and I'll take care of that while you do the other things," Carrie said. "I may be a capable adult, but I'm not ready to milk a goat yet."

"Do you think you will ever be?" Shea teased.

"Who knows?" Carrie said, raising her coffee mug. "Maybe someday."

They headed to the goat pen first. Shea pointed out the feed sacks inside the adjacent metal barn and told Carrie how much to give the bleating furry creatures, as well as how to go about filling the water troughs. While Carrie was busy with the feed, Shea opened the gate to the goat pen and found her milking stool. She led Annabelle to the milking stall first and sat down, reaching under the goat. While her hands moved with quick and quiet precision, Shea glanced through the slats of the stall and watched her daughter make the rounds with the feed. She bit her lip to prevent herself from laughing out loud when Carrie dumped half of the container on the ground outside of the fence on her first try and stood, perplexed, staring at the pile of wayward grain. After considering the mess for a moment, she simply shrugged and went back into the barn for a refill.

Carrie's now-positive attitude made Shea's heart swell with pride. As much as she had loved the idea of the twins finally coming to Oklahoma after two years, she'd been apprehensive about how they might react to her extremely different life. Carrie in particular.

But now she was here, trying and learning. It was a much better outcome than Shea had imagined.

Seven goats ran toward Carrie when she entered the pen. "Uhhh…Mom," she said, freezing in her tracks, her eyes wide.

"Don't worry, they won't hurt you," Shea assured her. "They just think they're starving every morning."

"Soooo…what do I do?"

"Act like you are in charge," Shea replied. It was the same advice Trish had given her when she'd first brought the goats home to the farm from the auction where she'd purchased them. "Walk right through the middle of them without hesitating – they'll get out of your way - and put the grain in the feeder."

"Alrighty then." Carrie took a deep breath and walked through the goats like she owned the place. She dumped the grain into the feeder and stood back as the goats crowded in around it, then turned and smiled as the youngest goats came prancing joyously toward her.

"Oh, my gosh! They're so cute!" She bent down and gingerly stroked them between the ears.

"Don't bend over Carrie," Shea blurted, rising halfway up from the stool. Carrie stood up and whirled around just in time to see a small billy goat named Bopsy rise up on his hind legs and scramble in her direction.

"Whoa," Carrie shouted, hand outstretched, as she stood her ground.

"Are you okay?" Shea asked.

Carrie cracked up as the little goat snorted, then turned and went on his way as though nothing had happened.

"I'm fine," she gasped, between guffaws. "Did you see that little guy? He was so serious. Like he thought he was a raging bull or something. Oh, my gosh, that was the cutest thing I've ever seen."

"Right?" Shea grinned, more than familiar with the baby goat's antics. She finished milking Annabelle and moved on to the second goat. When she looked out again, she saw Carrie sitting on a tree stump with two of the baby goats in her lap.

The milking finished, Shea carried the pails of fresh milk to the barn fridge. Carrie asked where the chicken feed was stored and headed to the chicken coop to feed the birds after Shea gave her the directions.

"Oh, and by the way, Carrie," Shea called out. "Watch out for the rooster. His name is Clarence and he's as ornery as the day is long," she warned.

"Got it," Carrie replied, letting herself into the coop. "Get back," she hollered, making Shea laugh. Clearly, she'd encountered Clarence. Shea joined her in the coop so that they could split the task of collecting the eggs and making sure that the chickens had plenty of clean water and straw.

Chris joined them in the kitchen just after six and apologized that he hadn't been awake to help with chores. "I'll help you tonight when we get back," he promised, placing his empty coffee mug in the sink and heading upstairs to get dressed.

"Do I have time for a shower?" Carrie asked.

"I hope so," Shea teased. "I'm going upstairs to take one."

"Who made the coffee? It's awful." She overheard Chris complain when she left the bathroom. Carrie's reply was unintelligible, but her tone was unmistakable. Shea smiled. She'd raised an independent young lady who wasn't at all afraid to defend herself.

Thirty minutes later, clean and refreshed, they were on their way west in search of the fish hatchery called Fisher's Local.

"Do you guys want to stop for a coffee on the way?" Shea asked.

"Do you even have to ask?" Carrie grinned. "I would die for a good latte."

"Told you that stuff you made this morning was terrible," Chris said, with a wicked smirk.

"Mom drank it," Carrie pointed out.

"Mom also ate the peanut butter, pickle, and pop tart sandwiches we used to give her when we were six," Chris reminded her.

"That's fair," Carrie replied, nodding.

"Hey, I still eat pickles with my pop tarts," Shea said with a wide grin.

She pulled into the parking lot of the coffee shop and took their orders. In just fifteen minutes, she returned to the Jeep with three large lattes and a bag of pastries.

"I am never going to survive Oklahoma at this rate," Carrie said, pulling a chocolate scone out of the bag.

"Do you want me to drive, Mom?" Chris asked, before Shea got back into the driver's seat.

"Yep, be my guest," Shea said. She set her phone on the dashboard so that she and Chris could hear the directions to the fish farm, then settled back into the passenger seat, grateful that someone else was doing the driving.

"So, what do we know about this fish place?" Carrie asked, leaning forward between the two front seats. "I mean, what was Dylan's actual complaint about them again?"

"I think it was selling bad fish, charging him too much," Chris said. "That kind of thing."

"Do you recall if there was a response from the fish farm? Did they ever call it out?" Shea asked. "We know that they were tagged in the posts, which means that they're aware of what Dylan had said, if they ever check their social media pages."

"I didn't get quite that far," Chris replied, preoccupied with driving.

"Most platforms either email you or send you some kind of notification when you get tagged in something anyway," Carrie said.

"Yeah, that makes sense. Hey, do you have your phone on you?" Shea asked.

"That's a given," Carrie replied. "Why? What do you need?"

"I was wondering if the fish farm has had other reviews," Shea said. "Chris is using my phone for directions, or I would have looked it up myself."

"Sure, hang on," Carrie said, digging in her small purse for her phone. "Okay, what's it called again?"

"Fisher's Local," Shea replied.

"Okay, cool. I'm looking," Carrie said, gazing down at her phone. Shea could hear the taps as she typed into the internet search bar. "Oh. Hmm…that's weird." She frowned.

"What's weird?" Chris asked, glancing in the rearview mirror.

"I can't find any reviews," Carrie said, looking puzzled.

"Did you look on Yelp? Or Google?" Chris suggested.

"Hang on," Carrie said, continuing to scroll. "Okay, I see a profile of the company on both, but it says that reviews have been locked."

"Locked?" Chris repeated. "I don't think I've ever seen reviews locked before."

"Same thing on their social media platforms," Carrie said, switching screens with a few clicks. "The posts are locked. The comments are locked. There's nothing recent posted, either."

Shea gazed out at the road, thinking, as Chris drove. She was intrigued about the things they were finding out about the fish farm. Maybe Dylan's posts hadn't actually been seen by the owners. While it was a bit odd to not advertise reviews far and wide, it wouldn't be the first time a company chose to have a minimal internet presence. It crossed her mind at that point that they could be wasting an entire morning on a wild goose chase. Shea sighed inwardly. She definitely could have used the day to catch up on the never-ending list of extra things that needed to be done around the farm.

"I think I have to turn left up here," Chris said, looking for confirmation.

Shea checked the screen of her phone and nodded. "Yep. It says turn left, then go right, go right again, and the fish farm should be at the bottom of the hill."

Chris slowed when he made the last turn and Shea noticed a faded billboard. On the company website, the words "Fisher's Local " had appeared to be a vibrant teal color, but on the sign they were sun-bleached a dim greenish-grey that made them nearly invisible.

"Are you sure this is it?" Shea asked, a slow curl of unease building in her midsection.

"I mean, how many of these things with the same name could there be?" Chris asked as he pulled into a large, empty parking lot in front of a large metal building surrounded by several square-shaped ponds, four on each side. Fenced walkways surrounded and divided each of the ponds. Tall windows lined the front of the building, spaced twenty feet apart.

"It looks dark inside," Carrie commented. "Are you sure it's even open?"

"Oh, you know what," Shea said, shaking her head. "I forgot that today is Sunday. It's probably not even open on the weekends."

"I don't know, something seems…off," Chris said, frowning slightly. He got out of the Jeep and walked up the sidewalk toward the first long window, then turned and motioned for Shea to join him.

A horrific, sickly-sweet odor grew increasingly stronger as she approached the building. She swallowed hard as bile threatened to rise in the back of her throat.

"What is that awful stench?" she asked, making a face.

"Look in the window," Chris told her, his eyes grave. Shea cupped her hands around the sides of her eyes and leaned against the glass, squinting. She saw nothing at first. Her eyes couldn't focus past the glare of the sun into the darkened building. But then, slowly, the picture began to come into focus. The expansive interior was filled with nothing but open space and dingy concrete floors.

"I think there may be offices over this way," Chris said. He moved down to the next window and looked in. "I can see a little bit of furniture, but nothing else."

Shea followed and peered in the second window as well. As soon as her eyes adjusted, she saw a long folding table and a few chairs scattered around what looked like it might have been a break room. On the far left she saw a few open office doors, but they were just as dark and empty as the first area had been.

"I don't think there is a fish farm here anymore," Carrie said from the sidewalk. "It even looks like the locks on the doors have been removed."

Shea backed away from the window and looked where Carrie was pointing. There were two large holes where locks had once been, in a pair of gray metal doors to the right.

"I don't think we should go inside," Carrie said, looking disgusted and holding one hand to her nose.

"Agreed," Shea replied. "We have no idea what might be behind those doors once we get past what little we can see, and we definitely don't need to be charged with trespassing."

"Are we trespassing now?" Carrie asked, brows raised.

"No. We're merely discovering that the fish farm has closed," Shea replied. "And the best thing that we can do at this point is to get back in the Jeep and leave."

"Looks like this place has been shut down for a long time, Mom," Chris said. "I want to take a look around back."

"Wait...are you thinking of walking back there, or driving?" Carrie asked, shooting a worried look at her mother.

"Driving, definitely. Let's get back in the car," Chris said, doing exactly that without waiting for a response.

There was a smaller parking lot beside the massive metal structure when they turned the corner. A pair of truck bays were situated in the middle of that side of the building. Shea noticed the "loading zone" sign painted on the asphalt below. The paint was still bright yellow, not faded like the old sign on the road had been.

Chris followed the parking lot all the way to the back of the building, and then turned around when the asphalt ran out.

"There aren't any trash bins left outside," he observed. "I would imagine that means the bills stopped getting paid, so the sanitation company already picked up their dumpsters."

"But it's not like this place hasn't been open in years," Shea said, scanning the surrounding area. "You can tell that by the bright yellow paint back there on the loading zone."

"Maybe they shut down after Dylan Branch posted his heinous review about them," Carrie suggested.

"Which means that we're going to have to find out who was in charge, because they might have had quite the axe to grind with Dylan," Shea said grimly.

CHAPTER SEVEN

"The fish farm is out of business," Chris said, looking at his phone before leaving the parking lot of what used to be Fisher's Local. "I found another listing on Google, and it says that it's permanently closed."

"Can you tell when it shut down?" Shea asked.

Chris shook his head. "No, but the last reviews were from about eight months ago."

"Wait, you found reviews?" Carrie asked.

"I found the fact that they exist, but I can't read the actual reviews," Chris replied. "I can see the dates and who left the review, but that's it."

"Interesting. I think we need to go home and regroup," Shea suggested. "It's going to be lunch time soon."

"Hey, Mom," Carrie said, leaning between the seats again. "Have you ever heard of a place called 'Pappy Jacks?'"

Shea shook her head. "I don't think so. What is it?"

"It's a diner, and they serve all sorts of fish," Carrie replied. "Are you guys ready for lunch?"

"What are you up to?" Chris asked.

"I think we should go and check out this fish place," Carrie said. "Maybe they'll have a little insight on the local fish scene…from an insider's perspective." She smiled slyly.

"How far away is it?" Shea asked.

"It's only about ten minutes from here," Chris replied. "And it doesn't look like a terrible place at least."

"Not terrible sounds good enough for me," Shea said.

"Alrighty then," Chris said.

Pappy Jack's turned out to be far more popular than the online reviews had indicated. At eleven in the morning, the parking lot was already packed. The tables that lined the large plate glass windows that ran across the front of the building were filled with people enjoying an early lunch.

"Wow, it's pretty busy for a restaurant that only opened thirty minutes ago," Shea observed, scanning the interior as they waited for the hostess to finish with a couple in front of them.

"So I guess that means it was a good choice." Carrie shrugged.

They were seated at a booth a few minutes later with menus in hand and glasses of ice water in front of them. Their server, a bubbly woman with dark hair pulled back into a bun, promised to return in a few minutes to take their order. While they read over the menu another server approached and left a basket of warm biscuits in the middle of the table along with a tub of butter and a bottle of honey.

"I see fried fish, fried fish, and more fried fish," Carrie said.

"Let's have some fried fish, then," Chris replied. "Come on, sis. Be a good sport. You'll have time to cleanse your arteries later."

"I see a grilled trout," Shea commented.

"I think I'll have the sampler platter," Chris announced. "But I'd really like to try the fried dill pickles."

"Order them as an appetizer," Shea suggested. "And I think I'll get the platter, too. Why not? I mean, if we're going to try to get some information about Fisher's Local, we might as well go big or go home."

Their server returned a moment later and took their orders. Much to Shea's surprise, Carrie ordered the sampler platter and Chris looked pleased when Shea added a basket of fried pickles.

"I can't believe you got the platter," Shea couldn't help but comment, when the server took their menus and returned to the kitchen.

"I figured when in Rome, get the oiliest thing on the menu," Carrie replied.

"Just keep an open mind," Chris said in a low voice. "We might be pleasantly surprised."

The server returned with a plate of piping hot coin-sized fried pickle chips and two large dipping bowls filled with ranch dressing.

"Here goes nothing," Carrie said, eyeing the plate cautiously. She picked up a pickle, dunked it in the ranch, and popped it in her mouth. Her eyes widened in surprise. "Whoa. That's amazing," she exclaimed, clearly savoring the bite.

Shea tried one next. "Oh, wow. You weren't kidding, that's dangerously good," she agreed. "I think I could eat the entire plate." Five minutes after they polished off the fried pickles, their server and another server returned with three large platters of food. Shea marveled at the mountain of food on her plate when it was set in front of her. There were at least ten pieces of fish, along with three hush puppies, a pile of fried okra, two pieces of corn on the cob, and another biscuit.

"I'm going to be eating on this for a couple of days," Chris commented. "What about you, Carrie? You probably have enough food there for a week for you and one of your goofy friends back at Mizzou," he teased.

"Probably," Carrie agreed, staring at her plate and shaking her head. She used her fork to cut off a piece from one of the large filets and took a bite. She chewed thoughtfully, then nodded. "Turns out I actually like fried fish."

"What kind of fish is this one, though?" Chris asked, pointing his fork at one of the thicker planks of fish. "I think it's supposed to be catfish."

"How is everything?" a manager in a crisp white shirt and a tie asked, approaching their table.

"It's really delicious," Shea replied.

"Well, I'm glad that you folks are enjoying it. My name is Dan – I'm the manager here, and I always like to hear from happy customers. Is this your first time at Pappy Jack's?"

"Sure is," Chris said with a broad smile. "Can you tell me what kind of fish I'm eating? I hate to admit it but I'm not sure what's on my plate."

"Well, over there by the okra, you have bass, next to that is trout, then perch, and finally catfish," Dan explained.

"Are these all local?" Chris asked. "I mean, I was just wondering if this is what is available around here. I'm from Arizona." Shea was impressed with her clever son.

"Yeah, I'm curious, too," Carrie added.

"Absolutely. Everything is locally sourced here," Dan replied.

"We were just down at the old Fisher's Local place earlier," Shea said. "We were a little shocked that it closed down."

"Fisher's Local. Hmm.." Dan's face clouded. "Are y'all some sort of food distributors or something? Restaurant owners?"

"Oh, no." Shea shook her head. "We were just hoping that maybe we'd be able buy some fresh fish from them. But then, when we saw that they were closed down, my son found this place online and we headed straight here."

"Oh." The manager seemed to relax. "So you folks must not have heard that there was a bunch of trouble here a few months ago," he said in a low voice.

"With Fisher's Local?" Shea asked.

"You betcha," Dan replied. He braced himself on the edge of their table and leaned in. "The owner of the place, Bobby Tarwater, was caught swapping mass market frozen filets for locally raised catfish. A couple of food critics caught on to what was happening, as well as one or two restaurant owners, and there was a huge scandal."

"What happened when they found out?" Shea asked.

"There was an investigation," Dan said. "Tarwater looked like he was going to be a stand-up guy and do the right thing. He lowered his head and admitted that what he'd done was wrong. But it wasn't too long before he went right back to what he'd been doing, until one of those other restaurant owners caught him in the act. Turns out he was doing other shady things behind the scenes, like passing bargain bin shrimp off as gulf shrimp that had been flown in the same day."

"Wow. How did they catch him?" Chris asked.

"There was one restaurant owner who could tell that the catfish filets were actually mass market," Dan said. "Apparently, he knew that the frozen filets were mushy in the middle and curled at the ends when they were fried. Fresh, local catfish doesn't do that. But what really sunk the ship for Fisher's Local was when some shrimp Tarwater sold to a guy in Tulsa sickened an entire group of Baptists at a church function."

"And the health department shut him down after that?" Shea asked.

"Yes ma'am, with a vengeance." Dan nodded, looking around as if to verify that he wasn't being overheard by other customers. "After that, Tarwater tried to burn the place down. He got caught and is headed to trial in January for attempted insurance fraud. I heard he lost his home, too."

Shea sipped her water and tried to think of what to say next. "Well, I guess that explains why the place was shut down when we tried to visit."

"Yep, and why Fisher's Local will never be opened again." Dan agreed, straightening up to a normal standing position. "You folks let Nettie know if you need anything. Enjoy the rest of your meal."

After exchanging a mildly surprised glance with each other, Shea and the twins ate the rest of their meal with little conversation as they mulled over what they'd just heard. They carried what they couldn't finish home with them in large boxes.

They were roughly halfway home when Shea's comfortably full feeling turned into a churning of her stomach that threatened to get ugly. She asked Chris to pull into a gas station and ran inside. When she came back to the Jeep, weak and nauseated, she discovered that it was empty. She wondered if Carrie and Chris had run inside as well.

"Did the food make us sick?" Carrie asked when she made her way outside, looking pale and unsteady.

"I don't think so," Shea replied. "It might just be that we're not used to eating that much fried food. It tasted great and the fish seemed fresh."

"Can you imagine what those people at that church function went through if they ate bad shrimp?" Chris said, shaking his head.

"Ugh," Carrie groaned. "That had to be beyond awful."

"I think we need to check into this Bobby Tarwater guy," Shea said. "He definitely seems like a solid potential suspect."

CHAPTER EIGHT

Back at the farm, Shea made room in the refrigerator for their lunch leftovers, although she wasn't sure if she'd actually eat the rest of the heavy fried food. A long nap sounded like heaven at the moment, but she was determined to continue to make some progress in Dylan's case now that they'd made the trip to the fishery and the restaurant.

Of course, one of the first things that she needed to find was Bobby Tarwater. Despite the information they heard from Dan, the manager at Pappy Jack's, she needed more to go on than just rumors and speculation. The fact that the fish farm was closed backed up the restaurant manager's story, but there might be more to the story that could shift the focus away from Bobby being a suspect. The former owner was almost certainly angry that he'd been caught doing shady deals, but was he angry enough with Dylan Branch to commit murder?

Shea ran upstairs to change her clothes so that she could run out to the garden and pick the ripe vegetables that she'd need for the following morning.

While she was changing, she could hear the sweet sounds of activity below her and smiled. Pulling her hair up into a ponytail, she waited, listening, for a moment in front of the mirror. A long time ago, in what seemed to be another world, she'd heard the same sort of moving around and talking to each other kinds of noises from the twins when they were still teenagers. But they were here now, in a new house in a new state and an entirely new lifestyle. Just the thought of it, and of how far she'd come, both personally and in her relationship with the twins, brought tears to Shea's eyes. She hoped that one or both of them would consider returning to the farm a little more often than they had in the past. Her new normal was looking a bit brighter now that they were on board.

She headed back down the stairs and into the kitchen where Carrie stood in front of the sink with a glass of water and Chris gazed out of the window.

"What are you up to now, Mom?" Chris asked, when he turned and noticed her somewhat well-used attire.

"I'm going to head out to the garden right now because I'd like to get ready for tomorrow and have the farm chores done a little early," Shea replied, hoping that they might want to keep her company.

"Same chores as before? Picking veggies, feeding the animals?" he asked.

"I'm also going to check for eggs and see if the girls are ready to milk," Shea said. "But yep, same chores as before."

"Okay. I'll check the chicken coop and then start picking in the tomato section, if that works for you," Chris volunteered.

"And I'd really like to try milking this time," Carrie added.

"That sounds great," Shea said, hiding the surge of joy that she felt. "It'll make things go so much faster."

While Chris gathered the eggs, Shea walked Carrie through the process of milking Annabelle, the calmer of the two nanny goats. She caught on so quickly that Shea decided to leave her on her own while she refilled the water and feed for the goats.

Roughly an hour later, Chris, Carrie, and Shea gathered in the garden shed to stash the freshly picked vegetables and eggs in the fridge.

"I think you need another one," Chris commented, staring into the fridge.

"Another what?" Shea asked.

"Fridge. You're running out of room in this one. You need two."

"Nah, we'll be fine," Shea replied. "We'll just run the excess crates down to the fridge that's in the farm stand."

"Do I get to drive the tractor this time?" Carrie asked.

"Oh, boy." Chris rolled his eyes. "I'll walk down, thanks. I've seen how you drive."

Carrie steered the tractor down the driveway just fine, but Shea winced every time she ground the gears along the way and was relieved when Carrie slipped into the proper parking space behind the farm stand without a hitch. They quickly unloaded the flatbed and had to do some clever arranging to pack the vegetables into the oversized fridge. When they were done, Chris announced that he'd be driving them back up the driveway, muttering something about his sister dropping a transmission like a hot potato.

Shea had just stepped out of the farmstand when she heard a vehicle approaching.

"Who is that?" Carrie asked, shielding her eyes against the sun with her hand. She nodded toward the maroon pickup truck that was slowing to turn into the driveway.

"It's Seth," Shea replied, wondering why he'd popped in without calling or texting. She hoped nothing was wrong. "That's his personal vehicle."

"You ready to head back to the house, Carrie?" Chris nodded to the sheriff and climbed up in the cab of the tractor.

"I guess we should leave you two alone," Carrie whispered to her mother when Seth approached. Shea raised an eyebrow at her and she dashed to the tractor and climbed aboard.

"How's it going?" Seth asked, after greeting Shea with a smile that made her feel warm from head to toe. He watched the tractor heading back toward the farmhouse.

"Actually, it's been pretty amazing," Shea replied. "It's good to see you here in the middle of the day, but I'm wondering what made you drive all the way out here," she said, tilting her head to gaze up at him.

"Well, I wish I could say that it was just because I needed a dose of that pretty smile, but unfortunately, while that's true too, I wondered if you could do me a favor," Seth said.

Shea felt a blush rising in her cheeks but decided to play it cool. "I guess that just depends on what the favor might be."

"Understandable," Seth replied easily. "We're finished with the crime scene at the bistro, but there are quite a few vegetables and produce in the kitchen that are about to go bad as you can well imagine."

"So you want me to come in and clean up the kitchen for you?" Shea frowned.

"No, not at all." Seth shook his head. "I was actually wondering if you could just gather up the vegetables and maybe bring them back out here for your compost bin or something, so they don't go to waste. I have a couple of other people handling the food from the walk-in coolers and other perishables. But I wanted someone I could trust in there."

"Which means you wanted me to do it so that you wouldn't be inviting in someone who might be a potential suspect," Shea translated, thinking aloud. "That tells me that you might be considering one of the distributors as a suspect."

"You know I can't talk about an ongoing investigation, even with the prettiest girl in the county," Seth said, the sparkle in his eyes moderating his warning tone.

"Of course I know that," Shea replied, trying to hide the flutter in her pulse that his words had caused. "But I'd be happy to reciprocate by telling you what I know about Organix Solutions," she offered coyly. "It's just an informed hunch, but I feel like there may have been a reason they were angry with Dylan."

Seth's brows rose and a look of concern passed over his features. "How do you know about Organix Solutions?" he asked.

"Chris is some kind of computer whiz, and he found a social media account that Dylan used under a pseudonym," Shea replied. "Apparently, Dylan used that account to call out a lot of people he had issues with."

"Your son found that?" Seth asked. "Did he find anything else?"

"Yep. There's at least one other person who may have been pretty mad at Dylan," Shea replied.

"Shea, I know that there's a delicate balance here, right now, and I don't want to interfere with your kids' visit home, but I really need to see that account," Seth said. "I've got a district attorney and a police chief who seem pretty convinced that since McKenna Lambert had a motive to kill her uncle and take over his business, she has to be the perpetrator. If there's a chance that it could be someone else, I need to know about it, because my gut tells me that it isn't her."

"Yeah, that's kind of what I thought too. For one thing, it's just too darn easy and these things are never that easy. Come on up to the house and I'll have Chris show you what he found," Shea replied.

"That's a long walk," he joked. "Hop on in the truck with me and we can drive up."

"I like the way you think, Sheriff."

When Seth pulled up in front of the house, Chris and Carrie rushed away from the window, pretending that they hadn't been watching the whole time. Shea bit her lip and tried to hold back the laughter that had bubbled up and was threatening to send her into gales of guffaws. The twins might be closing in on their twenty-first birthday, but clearly, they were just as nosy and curious as they'd been at ten.

"Hey, there," Seth greeted Chris when he walked into the kitchen. "Sorry for barging in on your family visit, but I had a couple of questions for you."

"Yeah?" Chris glanced at his mother for approval and she nodded. "What can I help you with?"

"Your mom mentioned a social media profile that you found belonging to Dylan Branch," Seth said. "Can you show it to me? From what she said, there may be some very important information pertaining to the murder case on that page."

"Yeah, no problem," Chris said, seeming to relax a bit. "Mom, can we use your laptop again?"

"Of course," Shea replied. "Let's move this party down to my office."

"Can you explain to me how you found it?" Seth asked. "I need to be able to establish that the profile is actually his."

Chris hesitated. "That depends. How much do you know about computers?" he asked.

"Enough to get by, usually," Seth replied. He followed Chris down the hall to the office and Shea busied herself in the kitchen, fixing cold drinks for the four of them.

"What did you tell him?" Carrie asked, keeping her voice low.

"He asked for me to come in and remove some of the vegetables from the bistro before they go completely rotten. We'll put them in the compost bin here," Shea explained. "Then he said something about the fact that he'd found other people to deal with the perishables in the coolers and freezers, and when I realized that he had to have meant he found distributors to do it, I mentioned that I knew about Organix Solutions."

102

"And he wanted to know how," Carrie said. Shea nodded, placed four frosted glasses on the tray, and headed into the living room. From there, she could hear the murmur of conversation between Chris and Seth in the office.

"Mom," Chris called out, a moment later. "Where did you go?"

"Living room," Shea said. "With cold drinks."

"Did he show you his black magic?" Carrie asked when Seth and Chris came down the hall a few seconds later.

"He showed me something," Seth replied. "I'm not sure I could reproduce it, but it's enough for my purposes in the investigation. I am also very interested in your visit to the other side of the state today."

"Is somebody in hot water for her snooping?" Carrie smirked.

"Don't act like we weren't a part of it," Chris said, giving his sister a look.

"Y'all found some very important information that may have given me a much-needed lead," Seth said. "But I would definitely advise you not to try to meet up with someone in person who could be responsible for a murder." There was a smile on his face, but steel in his gaze. "Now, do y'all think you can stop by the bistro this evening to pick up the vegetables?"

"Sure, we can do that," Carrie replied.

CHAPTER NINE

After Seth left, Shea filled the back of her Jeep with as many empty buckets and other containers as she could find. She searched the garden shed for three pairs of gloves, a pair for herself and one for each of the twins.

"Why are we going after old vegetables again?" Carrie asked when she climbed in the passenger seat.

"Because the food is going to start to rot long before the matter of who gets the bistro after Dylan's death is resolved," Shea replied. "And probably even before they figure out who killed him."

"I suppose his employees are also possible suspects," Carrie said, nodding.

Chris settled into the seat behind her and Shea drove to town, parking her Jeep behind Farm to Fork. She texted Andrea when she arrived and waited for the deputy to open the back door to allow them to come in with the empty containers. Shea followed Andrea inside, her eyes darting to and fro, looking for anything that might be out of place. The pungent smell of bleach stung the inside of her nose.

"The cooler with the vegetables is over on the right," Andrea said, pointing to a large stainless-steel door.

Shea pulled it open, donned her gloves, and began removing the vegetables from the wire shelves. She recognized that most of the produce had come from her stand and a wave of sadness washed over her, but she didn't indulge it. She had to keep a clear head. There was work to be done and a crime to solve.

"Why didn't they just throw this stuff away?" Chris asked. He placed three large zucchinis in the bucket he carried and started filling in the empty spaces with onions and tomatoes.

"This stuff doesn't smell very good," Carrie complained, wrinkling her nose.

"No, it doesn't, and it isn't getting any fresher," Shea replied. She filled one bucket and began working on the second. "And to answer your question, Chris, it's possible that the police haven't been able to let anyone else in here to do it. It's also possible that there isn't anyone left to pay for the trash bill. If the vegetables are left outside, they could become a public health issue."

Chris nodded. "Yeah, that makes sense."

They filled all of the containers they'd brought and took them back to the Jeep. When they were done, Shea went back inside and looked around for Andrea. She walked slowly through the massive kitchen and stopped just outside a door that led to what appeared to be a large storage room. Tall wire shelving lined the walls, and the door had been propped open with a wooden wedge. Shea peered inside and her eyes burned as the smell of bleach nearly knocked her over.

Clearly, she'd found the murder scene, and she definitely didn't want to hang out there.

She turned swiftly back to the doorway and came nose to nose with McKenna Lambert. Her face was red and swollen from crying. "Oh, McKenna," Shea murmured. It was a nurturing instinct that she couldn't overcome and didn't want to. Without even thinking twice, she reached for the girl and pulled her into a hug.

"I can't believe someone killed him," McKenna sobbed. "I swear I didn't do it. The police thought I did it at first, but I think they know better now."

"Did they tell you that you're no longer a suspect?" Shea asked, pulling back and handing McKenna the spare handkerchief that she always kept in her purse for emergencies.

McKenna nodded. "Yeah, they told me that my alibi checks out," she said, dabbing at her eyes and nose. "I know that they looked into my mother, too. She never had a decent relationship with Uncle Dylan." She held the handkerchief out to Shea.

"You just hold on to that – you may need it later. How's your mom?" Shea asked.

"Recovering from a car accident. She was in Colorado this week and some guy t-boned her," McKenna replied. "At first, when Mom was missing, the cops seemed to think that she might have been the one who killed my uncle."

"She was missing?" Shea asked.

McKenna nodded. "I knew that she'd been out of state. But it wasn't until the hospital called me after she was brought in from the car crash that I found out where she was."

"Is she okay?" Shea asked, hoping that yet another tragedy hadn't befallen upon the poor girl.

"She will be. They said she'd recover, but she had a lot of broken bones from the wreck. I have to figure out some way to get her back here when she's released from the hospital," McKenna said, shaking her head.

"You've got a lot going on," Shea sympathized.

"Yeah, you can say that again." She snorted and wiped at her nose.

"McKenna, do you know anything about a food distribution company called Organix Solutions? I think Dylan might have called them out online and I wondered if you might have heard anything about them," Shea asked carefully, making her way out of the storage room so her eyes would stop burning.

McKenna leaned against the outside of the doorway and sighed. "I know he had quite a few fired up phone calls with those people," she said. "He found out that the products they sent us weren't organic like they were supposed to be."

"What products were they? Do you remember?"

"I don't remember everything, but I think the black beans for the black bean burgers that we make turned out to be non-organic. Same with some of the veggie wraps. There were a ton of things they were bringing here and charging a lot of money for that turned out not to be organic," McKenna said. "And the other bad thing about them was that some of the stuff they brought in ended up being out of date and spoiled."

"Oh, that's awful," Shea replied, making a face. "Was there ever any kind of physical confrontation?"

McKenna nodded. "One day a couple of months ago, a delivery driver started yelling at Dylan because he was looking at every expiration date on a delivery of garbanzo beans. I think that guy was really mad at him, but he quit and went to work in Texas, I think. I told the police all of that stuff."

"I'm sure that you did. But you know, sometimes, someone who is more of an outsider can help you see the forest through the trees."

"Look, I know Uncle Dylan wasn't the easiest person to work for or get along with. I guess I know that better than most. But there is one thing he did know, and that was this business," McKenna continued sadly. "He got an offer to run this really bougie restaurant in New Orleans, ya know."

"I hadn't heard that," Shea replied. "Why didn't he move to Louisiana, then?"

McKenna smiled, then bit her lip and took a big breath before responding. "It's this place. His home. He grew up here. His parents are buried here. And now he will be," she said, her words trailing away.

"I'm so sorry for your loss, McKenna," Shea said softly. "I think there are lots of people who know that Dylan opened Farm to Fork to help the small farmers around here. I'm pretty sure that's why he was so hard on me when I first moved here." She smiled faintly, remembering, then shook her head. "He wasn't about to let me into the club until I proved myself."

The corners of McKenna's mouth turned up slightly. "You might not believe this, but I heard him brag about your produce, you know. I heard him telling one of his customers one day what a great job you'd done with the farmer's market, too," she said.

"Really? That both shocks me to my foundation and touches me deeply." Shea swallowed past the lump in her throat.

"Right? He definitely wasn't one to go around tossing out compliments," McKenna agreed. "I remember hearing him talking about how you and your friend figured out how that old lady at the farmer's market didn't really kill her husband like everyone was saying. And you helped Uncle Dylan, when the cops were messing with him, too."

"I wish I could help him again, McKenna. Just one last time. That's why I'm wracking my brain to figure this out," Shea admitted. "He wouldn't want you getting blamed for something you didn't do."

"Geez - what's taking you so long, Mom?" Carrie asked, popping into the kitchen. She saw Shea and

McKenna at the door of the storeroom and stopped. "Oh, I'm sorry, I didn't mean to interrupt. Mom, is everything okay?" she asked, giving McKenna the onceover.

"Yeah, we're fine," Shea replied. She nodded toward McKenna. "This is Dylan Branch's niece, McKenna Lambert."

"Oh. Wow. I'm sorry about your uncle," Carrie said quietly. "How are you doing?"

"I'd be a lot better if we could figure out who did this to him and why," McKenna replied. "But thanks for asking."

Chris appeared behind his sister. "What's going on?"

"McKenna, this is my son, Chris," Shea said quickly. "He and Carrie are here on a break from school."

McKenna stared for a moment, looking from Chris to Carrie and back again. "You both look like your mom," she said, managing a small smile.

"Thanks," Chris replied, his expression curious.

"We should probably get going," Shea said, heading toward the door with Chris and Carrie at her heels.

McKenna stepped away from the storeroom door and seemed to be following them, when Shea heard Andrea Salt's voice. She figured the deputy must be standing by the back door waiting for them to leave.

Shea glanced back at the storage room one more time as she left, thinking how terrible it must have been for Dylan to meet his end there. She sighed, hugged herself around the middle, and kept staring at the door when something caught her eye.

Beneath the doorframe, tucked into a crack between the frame and the floor, she saw what looked like a folded up piece of white paper. Part of the paper appeared wrinkled from moisture. Shea stepped closer and reached down to pick it up. Despite its appearance, the paper was dry. She pulled it out slowly so that it wouldn't get damaged. The police must've missed it because they'd probably had the door wide open, which would have covered the paper's hiding place perfectly.

"Are you coming, Mom?" Chris called, making her jump guiltily.

"If you're ready to go, Shea, I would like to close this place back up," Andrea said from her spot outside the back door.

Shea shoved the piece of paper in her pocket and headed toward the door. "On my way," she called out as she went.

Shea said goodbye to Andrea and waited while Chris and Carrie settled back in their seats before pulling the thick piece of folded paper out of her pocket. Andrea locked the door and jogged over to her patrol car, pulling out of the parking lot as Shea began to examine the paper she'd discovered.

"What"s that?" Chris leaned forward and asked.

"I'm not sure. Could be something, could be nothing," Shea replied, carefully smoothing down the wrinkles in the piece of paper. "I found it under the door to the storage room." McKenna, whom Shea hadn't seen leaning against the back wall of the restaurant, stepped closer to watch.

"Looks like some kind of a receipt," Carrie said.

Shea smoothed the paper out. It was about eight inches long and three inches wide. She turned it over and squinted, using her cell phone flashlight to read the faded ink. "Oh, my gosh," she breathed.

"What? What is it, Mom?" Carrie asked.

"Hold on," Shea said, scanning it to look for a date. When she found it, she closed her eyes. "I think we might have just figured out who killed your uncle."

CHAPTER TEN

"I'm going to lose my mind if you don't start talking, Mom," Chris said from the back seat.

Shea held up the paper. "This is a receipt...from Pappy Jack's."

"What's Pappy Jack's," McKenna asked.

"It's a restaurant about an hour and a half from here," Shea replied. "We were just there and spoke with the manager about another person your uncle called out online."

"Why would a receipt from that place, of all places, be on the floor here?" Carrie asked. "That's an odd coincidence."

"Unless it isn't a coincidence," Shea said, thinking.

"We have no idea how long that's even been there, though," Chris said.

"I don't know about that," Shea replied. "Look at the edges. This was wet and recently dried. And the date on the receipt is less than one week ago."

"Y'all are gonna have to fill me in," McKenna said. "What in the world are you talking about?"

"We're thinking that someone we just met might not be who he says he is," Carrie explained, seeming to read Shea's mind.

"The manager of this restaurant might actually be a guy named Bobby Tarwater," Shea revealed.

"Bobby Tarwater? I know who he is," McKenna said, grimacing. "He's one of those lowdown swindlers that argued with my uncle over the phone."

"Have you ever met him in person?" Shea asked.

McKenna nodded. "Yep, I sure have. He used to come around, but that was over a year ago."

"Would you know him if you saw him again?" Chris asked.

"Yeah, I'd know him. Some people are so nasty you don't ever forget 'em, know what I mean?" McKenna said. "But I don't think he's around here anymore. My uncle said he got himself into a bunch of trouble and disappeared."

"Do you have time to go for a ride," Shea asked.

"You mean like, right now?" McKenna's brows rose.

Shea nodded. "Yes. Right now," she replied. "If we leave now, we can get there before Pappy Jack's closes."

"That's a long drive and we don't even know if the manager will be there, Mom," Chris pointed out.

"Well, it's easy enough to figure that out," Carrie replied. "Just pick up the phone and call the restaurant. Ask them if the manager is in, then, if he is, and they go to get him, hang up before he answers and drive like a bat out of Hades to the restaurant."

"I like the way you think," McKenna smiled, hoisting herself up into the back seat beside Chris.

"Put on your best snobby customer act and make the call, Carrie. Use my phone so they can't trace the call back to your number," Shea directed.

"Shouldn't be too much of a stretch," Chris commented. McKenna stifled a giggle.

"I know how to block the number," Carrie told Shea, ignoring her brother.

"Use mine anyway, honey," Shea insisted.

"Fine, whatever," Carrie said, rolling her eyes. She picked Shea's phone up from the console between the seats and searched for the number. Seconds later, she was dialing.

"Yes, I was in earlier this evening, and I would really like to speak to the manager, please," Carrie said, sounding uncomfortably much like one of the suburban housewives that used to be in Shea's social circle in Arizona.

"Who is that? Mrs. Polley or Mrs. Ratcliffe?" Chris asked, referring to two of Shea's former acquaintances.

"Certainly, this is Ariel De Salle," Carrie spoke again. "And to whom am I speaking?"

"She's good at sounding all high and mighty," McKenna whispered in the back seat. "I don't think there's anybody in town that sounds like that, other than your mama."

"Perfect, thank you. Are you the manager? Because I'd like to speak with the manager. Yes, I'll hold," Carrie said. She gave them a thumb's up and smiled, holding the phone between all of them, with a finger to her lips for quiet.

"This is Dan, how may I help you?" they heard, just before Carrie tapped the phone to end the call. "There, see. He's there right now, so let's hurry," Carrie urged.

"You got it," Shea said, backing out of her space and heading for the exit.

"Wow," Shea said. "You just hung up on him. Normally, I'd say that was rude." She chuckled.

"Couldn't happen to a nicer guy," Carrie said. She set the phone back down. "But it was him. We all heard him say his name was Dan and he sounded like the same guy."

"So, what's the plan now, Mom?" Chris asked, as they headed out of town, toward the highway. "Do we just go in, get a table, and see if McKenna recognizes him?"

"Something like that," Shea replied, pressing her foot down on the gas pedal. "We'll figure it out."

They were mostly silent for the long ride to the restaurant, but McKenna and Chris chatted quietly on occasion.

"Are we going to just walk in like we're all together?" McKenna asked, out of the blue.

"Yeah, you can be my date," Chris offered, with his most charming grin.

"Oh, brother," Carrie drawled.

"Just settle down, you two," Shea said, shaking her head. "We need to go in there with straight faces."

"I hate to be the one to point out the obvious, but shouldn't we call Sheriff Grayson or something before we do this?" McKenna asked.

"Yeah, we should," Shea said. "I probably should have done that in the first place."

"Carrie." Chris leaned forward. "Hand me Mom's phone."

"Why? What are you going to do?" Carrie handed him the phone.

Chris opened the phone and found Seth's number in the directory. "Sheriff Grayson, it's Chris Beaumont," he said. "No, Mom is fine. We just thought we should let you know we're headed back to Pappy Jack's restaurant near Oakmont. McKenna Lambert is with us. Mom found a receipt when we were at the restaurant earlier from Pappy Jack's."

Chris paused and listened for a moment. "No, it's just a hunch. The manager told us his name was Dan, but we're all pretty sure that it's Bobby Tarwater."

"Tell him McKenna knows what Tarwater looks like," Shea whispered.

"We have McKenna with us to identify him," Chris continued. "Okay, Okay. Yes, sir. Loud and clear." He hung up the phone and handed it back up to Carrie.

"Is he mad?" Carrie asked.

"Not at all," Chris replied. "He's less than thirty minutes away, too. He said he'll be there as soon as possible."

"There's something we should probably think about," McKenna said. "What are we going to do if Bobby Tarwater recognizes me?"

Shea searched in her console for the ball cap she kept in the car for hair emergencies. "Problem solved," she said, handing it back to McKenna.

"Thanks," McKenna said. She piled her long dark hair on top of her head and plopped the cap onto it, making sure that short ends hung out, giving her a short-haired look. Pulling the bill down low over her dramatic blue eyes, she hid her identity very effectively. "Better?" she asked.

"I barely recognize you," Shea said, pulling into the parking lot. "Here we go. Now, everyone just try to look relaxed and follow my lead."

They headed inside and waited to be seated behind a line of other diners.

"You guys look around and see if you spot him," Shea directed. "But be discreet. Don't be obvious."

"What if we do see him?" Carrie asked, pretending to examine her nails while looking around the restaurant.

"You quietly let McKenna know and then she can determine if he's Bobby Tarwater," Shea replied.

CHAPTER ELEVEN

Fortunately, they didn't have to wait to be seated before discovering Dan's identity. Shea glanced at the employee plaque on the wall behind the hostess station.

Daniel Smith was listed as the assistant manager.

"Original," Shea said, inclining her head toward the plaque.

"Over there," Chris leaned over to McKenna and whispered. "He's the one wearing a tie near that group of old ladies."

"I see him," McKenna said, turning pale. "That's him."

"Are you sure? We really need to be completely sure," Shea said. Her phone chimed. She turned it over to view the message on the screen. "Seth is here." The words filled her with relief.

"Oh geez, Mom, he's heading toward us," Chris whispered, turning his head away. "Maybe we should just leave."

"Absolutely. Let's go," Shea said, turning away and placing her arm around Carrie's shoulders. "Step lively, before he sees us."

McKenna took Chris's arm and headed for the door, with Carrie and Shea behind them.

"Hey, folks, are you leaving us so soon?" 'Dan' called out behind them. "Weren't you guys here earlier?"

"Keep walking," Shea murmured.

"Hey, hey," Dan said as he scurried over to head them off. "Hey, I know you! You, in the hat."

McKenna froze. "Sorry," she said, hiding her strong Oklahoma accent with a pitiful attempt at a British one. "Wrong person." She sounded a bit like Eliza Doolittle.

They power walked out of the restaurant, gulping in breaths of cooler evening air. Seth passed them halfway across the parking lot, surrounded by three uniformed officers from the local county. Once they were far enough away to stay out of the action, but watch through the large windows, Shea stopped, her arms folded, as Seth and his team went inside.

She watched as the waiting crowd of diners cleared out of the way so that Seth and the other officers could approach the manager. Dan whirled away, ducked his head, and tried to dash out of the front lobby area to disappear inside the restaurant. But, as fate would have it, a waiter with a round tray filled with fish platters blocked his exit. Cornered, Dan turned back and smiled.

"Can I help you officers this evening?" he asked, or at least that's what Shea imagined him saying, judging by his manner.

Shea smiled and opened the door of the Jeep.

"Mom," Chris said, still standing and watching the spectacle. "Where are you going?"

"Home," Shea replied. "I would imagine that the sheriff is going to want to speak with McKenna before the night is over. He'll need her to make an official identification and give her statement."

"You should probably get the receipt you found at the bistro and give it to the sheriff," Carrie reminded her.

"Already on it," Shea said. She reached in and grabbed the receipt from the cup holder in her door. "Whoa," she exclaimed.

"What's the matter?" Chris asked, immediately alert.

"Because it stinks really bad in there," Shea replied. She covered her mouth and nose with her free hand.

"The vegetables," Chris said, realization dawning.

"Oh, no," Carrie gasped. "I forgot all about them. What are we going to do?"

"Drive home fast, with the windows down," Shea said. She handed the keys over to Chris and went to meet Seth with the receipt when he stepped back outside.

CHAPTER TWELVE

"I think we make a really good team," Carrie said.

They were gathered at the farm for dinner to celebrate their last day before returning to central Missouri. She wrapped an arm around her mother and brother from behind, inserting herself into the middle. "We should solve murders together more often."

"I don't know that we can actually take credit for solving the murder," Chris said. "We just got lucky when we figured out that Dan from Pappy Jack's was actually Bobby Tarwater."

"Yeah, but we wouldn't have even known about Bobby Tarwater and Fisher's Local if we hadn't gone looking into things," Carrie replied.

"I'm fairly confident that the sheriff's department would have figured things out on our own eventually, thanks," Seth said, setting a large dish of potato salad on the picnic table.

"Yes, let's give the boys in blue the benefit of the doubt, please," Shea said, giving Carrie a look.

"What happened when you got him to jail?" Carrie asked Seth, winking at her mother.

"Not much. He started talking a whole lot about how he isn't who we think he is and then he talked even more about the pressures in the restaurant industry," Seth said. "Eventually he told us some story about going to Farm to Fork to convince Dylan to hire him as a manager. He swore that the meeting was friendly, and that he turned around and left afterwards."

"Did you release him?" Shea asked.

"Nope, not a chance," Seth replied. "We arrested him on second degree murder charges after he talked some more and told us that the conversation got a little heated when he told Dylan that he owed him a job because it was Dylan's fault that his fish farm shut down. He even managed to try and blame him for the arson at the fishery."

"Unbelievable," Chris said, shaking his head. "What did the prosecutor's office say?"

"Oh, they offered him a plea deal," Seth said. "Second degree murder rather than first degree. Thirty years to life instead of death row." He turned to Chris. "What's your major again?"

"Internet Technology," Chris said, placing a large blob of potato salad on his plate. "Why do you ask?"

"I was just wondering if you'd ever considered a career in law enforcement. You're pretty good at logically thinking and finding things."

Chris tilted his head to the side, eyebrows raised. "I've been talking to my academic counselor about a lot of different career options," he said. "But with my dad in federal prison, she made it seem as though I couldn't pursue a career in either law enforcement or in the military."

Seth shook his head. "That's a whole load of hogwash. One of the best federal agents I ever met was the son of a notorious swindler. There are ways around it. And I think you'd have a very bright future in law enforcement if you decided to go that way."

"Thanks, that's definitely something to think about," Chris said, a faraway look in his eyes.

"Listen, Chris," Seth said, reclaiming his attention. He took a seat across the table. "I mean this. If you decide that you'd like to pursue taking that career path, come and talk to me. I'll help you in any way I can. If that means you need me to travel to Columbia with your mom, we can make it happen. Letters of recommendation, anything you might need."

Shea glanced over at Chris and was delighted to see him smiling broadly as he reached across the table to shake Seth's hand. "Thank you, sir," he said. "That really means a lot to me."

Shea turned her attention to Carrie. "I bet you're anxious to get back to school," she said.

"Actually," Carrie said. "I have been thinking about going virtual."

"Going virtual?" Shea repeated.

"She means taking all of her classes online instead of going back to school in person," Chris translated. "I think it's actually a really cool idea."

"What do you plan to do?" Shea asked, turning back to Carrie.

"Well, I've been looking into it, and I still have time to switch the focus of my major a little," she replied. Her face turned pink as she spoke.

"What are you studying now?" Seth asked.

"Marketing, more or less. I've been working on a degree in communications," Carrie replied. "But I've decided to switch to journalism."

"Oh, that's wonderful, honey." Shea beamed.

"Tell them the rest of it, Carrie," Chris urged

"I will, geez," Carrie said, making a face at him. "I'm going to switch to ag journalism."

"What's that?" Shea asked.

"Agricultural journalism. I started looking into it at the end of my freshman year. When you moved here, I got really curious about farming and agriculture." Carrie shrugged.

"What made you decide to make the change?" Shea asked. She worked hard to keep her building enthusiasm in check as she spoke.

"Being here," Carrie said simply. "Spending time with you out in the fields and with the animals. It's really changed my perspective."

"So, what will that mean?" Seth asked. "Are you going back to Arizona? I would think that it would make more sense for you to come here and be with your mom on the farm."

Carrie reached her hand across the table and squeezed Shea's hand. "If you wouldn't mind, Mom," she said, shyly. "I think I'd like to relocate here and help you with the farmer's market while I finish school. After that? Who knows? Maybe I can find freelance work and hang around here for a while."

"You want to move here to the farm? Live here with me, permanently," Shea asked, feeling unshed tears beginning to sting her eyes.

Carrie looked off in the distance. She pursed her lips and squinted. "I was thinking about it, if you're okay with me moving in," she said. "I think I might like to give this farming life a go on a permanent basis. It seems to have worked out for you."

"I think that would be really really nice," Shea said. *Understatement of the year.*

"Well, I don't know about you guys, but I'm digging in," Chris said, surveying his plate with relish.

The twins put the food away and did the dishes after lunch, while Shea and Seth moved to the more comfortable chairs on the porch to digest their food and the good news.

"Well," Seth said after a second of rocking silently side by side. "I'm thinking that things have worked out just about perfectly," he said, gazing off toward the sunset. He reached for her hand and entwined his fingers with hers. "Things took a bit of a turn today, didn't they?"

"How do you mean?" Shea asked, enjoying the golden haze that was embracing the farm.

"Well, a few weeks ago you weren't sure the twins would even make the trip here to visit you. I remember hearing you wondering if they were blaming you for their father winding up in prison. And now, here you are with your daughter wanting to move here and make this her home, possibly forever. She's looking into a career change because of the life you've built here, Shea."

"The life I've built here," Shea repeated. "I like the sound of that."

Shea leaned against Seth's shoulder. "You know, I have to thank you for helping make the middle of nowhere Oklahoma feel like a home."

"Watch how you talk about my town now, girl," he warned playfully. "I'd hate to have to run you off."

"Not a chance." Shea laughed, snuggling closer.

"Nope, not a chance." Seth agreed, kissing the top of her head.

They could both see Chris and Carrie grinning as they peeked out from behind the curtain, but they pretended not to notice.

Check out all the books in Summer Prescott's catalog!

Summer Prescott Book Catalog

AUTHOR'S NOTE

I'd love to hear your thoughts on my books, the storylines, and anything else that you'd like to comment on—reader feedback is very important to me. My contact information, along with some other helpful links, is listed on the next page. If you'd like to be on my list of "folks to contact" with updates, release and sales notifications, etc.... just shoot me an email and let me know. Thanks for reading!

Also...

... if you're looking for more great reads, Summer Prescott Books publishes several popular series by outstanding Cozy Mystery authors.

CONTACT SUMMER PRESCOTT BOOKS PUBLISHING

Twitter: @summerprescott1

Bookbub: https://www.bookbub.com/authors/summer-prescott

Blog and Book Catalog: http://summerprescottbooks.com

Email: summer.prescott.cozies@gmail.com

YouTube: https://www.youtube.com/channel/UCngKNUkDdWuQ5k7-Vkfrp6A

And…be sure to check out the Summer Prescott Cozy Mysteries fan page and Summer Prescott Books Publishing Page on Facebook – let's be friends!

To download a free book, and sign up for our fun and exciting newsletter, which will give you opportunities to win prizes and swag, enter contests, and be the first to know about New Releases, click here: http://summerprescottbooks.com

Made in United States
Cleveland, OH
24 September 2025